CHEYANNE YOUNG

Evernight Teen ®

www.evernightteen.com

Copyright© 2023

Cheyanne Young

ISBN: 978-0-3695-0838-6

Cover Artist: Jay Aheer

Editor: CA Clauson

CHEYANNE YOUNG

DEDICATION

For Felicia,
and in memory of Dorothy (Granny) Morgan.

When I think of home, I think of you two.

CHEYANNE YOUNG

THE YEARS BETWEEN US

Cheyanne Young

Chapter One

The hatchback of my ten-year-old Mini Cooper groans open while I stand here in the pre-heated oven that is Texas, gazing into the tiny, tiny trunk. Little dots of glitter decorate the interior from last year's STEM project posterboard. And, well, every school project, because they all end up with glitter on them when I've finished. The weight of my broken heart seems to slog my muscles into moving slower, working harder. I heft my two overstuffed backpacks off the ground and heave them into the Cooper's miniscule trunk space.

Are two backpacks of clothes enough for the entire summer? Originally, no. Interning at the Starr Observatory would have called for garment bags, suitcases, and more than one pair of shoes so that I could go into work looking professional, like someone who deserves a college scholarship to study astronomy. But now, a small wardrobe of baggy shirts, shorts, one bathing suit, and my favorite flip flops fits perfectly into the theme of Emma Fitzgerald's life.

Everything in my life is small. This car. The backpacks. My college fund.

The amount of love Jonah had for me.

Just … small.

Too small.

My life is the smallest spec of glitter in the smallest car trunk in the sky. And sure, maybe my life is a roaring star in someone else's universe, a massive ball of fiery energy that keeps a far-away planet inhabitable, but certainly not in mine.

The shuffling sound of socks-in-slides on the concrete tells me Nina is approaching. She must have walked over or I would have seen her drive up since I'm facing the highway. Her neighborhood is just one trespassed yard and a gas station parking lot jaunt away from the motel where I live.

Living in The Infinity Motel is not as weird as it sounds. It's actually a bit weirder than it sounds. My parents and I live in an apartment converted from two motel rooms, and Uncle Ray and his husband live in the apartment below ours. My parents and uncles bought the Cypress Road Inn when I was a toddler and turned it into the world's nerdiest inn, where each room features a different theme from a beloved fictional fandom. Mom is obsessed with the Star Wars room, which is rented out more often than others, but the Dr. Who room is my favorite. The door is painted to look like the Tardis, and it only took me about three tries and a dozen YouTube video tutorials to get the paint job just right.

The Infinity Motel is fun and quirky and exactly everything my family stands for, but living with my parents in a motel is a tight fit. Unlike my cat, Mando, I'm not a fan of tight spaces.

I'm a comet, meant to be soaring through exciting new adventures, never staying still. That's why I'm leaving this summer. *Folks, if you keep an eye out, you'll see Emma Fitzgerald soaring through town tonight.*

Plus, every square inch of town reminds me of Jonah.

"Let me guess..." Nina says, standing beside me, surveying the inside of my trunk. "You're having some poetically philosophical conversation with yourself about how sucky your life is because one jerk broke your heart, and another jerk stole your dream summer job and now both of those jerks have combined their evil forces into one big romantic relationship?"

My best friend is several inches shorter than me, with a lean, athletic build, dark hair that's always in a low ponytail, and an entire wardrobe that matches mine, meaning it's pretty casual. She's wearing a tank top, black shorts, and those ugly pink foam slides she adores so much.

I heave a sigh. "Pretty much."

She snorts, then leans into the Mini Cooper and drops another backpack on top of mine.

"What's that?"

"My clothes. Phone charger. A batch of Abuela's homemade almond butter." She shrugs, counting on her fingers as she lists things. "Toothpaste. Deodorant. I shouldn't need tampons thanks to my IUD, but you never know, so we've got some of those, too."

"We?"

Her dark eyes light up. "I'm coming with you to Granny's for the summer. I've already texted her and she's cool with it."

The idea of Nina spending my summer exile with me at Granny's makes my broken insides feel like they might heal a little quicker. But the whole reason I chose to exile myself for the summer was so that my parents and best friend wouldn't be stuck with me while I sort out this damn broken heart. It's not every day a person loses their boyfriend and dream summer job to their mortal enemy. I don't know how else to heal myself besides running away to my grandmother's loving, extremely spoiling arms. Seriously, we're going to eat pizza and donuts every day. It's the Granny Ross way.

"What about hot girl summer?" I say, putting a hand on my hip. "Your plan to make out with as many hot girls as possible this summer won't go so well in Pine Grove. It has a population of, like, two thousand people and most of them are over sixty."

"Every summer has the potential to be hot girl summer." Nina wiggles her eyebrows. "I can miss this one."

"You're the best, you know that?"

She slams my trunk closed then winks at me. "Girl, I know."

Across the parking lot, Uncle Ray returns from his trip to Costco in our work truck that's loaded with cases of bottled water, drinks, and snacks for the motel. I wave at him. He rolls down the window, leaning out. "You gonna make me unload all of this by myself?"

"No, of course not," I call back. "That's what your husband is for!"

I've already said goodbye to the rest of my family, but I wasn't expecting my uncle to come back before I left. I toss my keys to Nina and ask her to start the air conditioner, then I jog over to Uncle Ray.

He's a couple years younger than my mom, but he looks older, with his slightly graying hair and the fine wrinkles across his forehead and in the corners of his eyes. My mom and uncle were both adopted, so while she's pale and freckled, he has light brown skin and dark hair that he keeps trimmed short. He's a huge fan of this CrossFit outdoor gym down the road, so he's in great shape.

"You're really leaving all summer?" he says, getting out of the truck.

"Yep. You guys already hired my temporary replacement, so I might as well enjoy my summer off."

Ray drops the truck's tailgate then leans over, lowering his voice to a conspiratorial whisper. "I don't really like that guy."

"But he's a huge nerd!" I protest. "That's why you hired him. He's perfect for the motel."

Ray rolls his eyes. "He's a little too much of a nerd. He's constantly trying to one-up me with Lord of the Rings facts. Like, dude, no one cares that you run an online forum for the Hobbitish language, which by the way, was lost in history, so what's the point?"

I laugh. "Sorry. I'll be back before you know it."

"Have a good summer," he says, pulling me into a quick hug. He kisses the top of my head. "And remember that all the stuff that seems to matter now, really doesn't matter. Not in the long run."

My heart twinges with the sudden reminder of all the things I'm running away from. I guess he's right. I guess maybe high school loves who crush your heart to pieces might not matter in ten years, but it matters now. It *hurts* now.

I wrap my arms around him, breathing in the familiar oceanic scent of his cologne. "I love you, Uncle Ray."

"Love you, too, kid."

He smiles at me in this tight-lipped, eyes-on-the-horizon way that looks like he wants to say something. But he doesn't, and I'm not really in the mood to hear more advice about broken hearts, so I jog back to my car where Nina has put on her favorite K-pop band and cranked the bass.

"Are you sure you don't want to take your car in case you get bored and want to go home early?" I ask, partly because I don't want her to be bored this summer, and partly because I really don't want to listen to K-pop for an hour. Old school punk rock is more my style. I take after my mom that way.

"Nah," she says, plugging her phone into my car charger. "This is our last summer before senior year. Next summer, who knows where we'll be. I want to spend every minute of summer with my best friend and her cool ass grandma."

"You really take all the fun out of being sad," I say, throwing up my arms in mock disgust. "You just show up here like a freaking ray of sunshine and make things all better. I won't have any fun moping around Pine Grove this summer."

"Sorry, Emma." Nina snorts. "I'm your best friend. This is literally my job."

****

Pine Grove is a teensy gulf coast country town in Texas, known for the killer humidity, ugly seaweed-covered beaches with brown water, and, well, that's all I can think of. Mom and Uncle Ray grew up here with their adoptive parents and then left for the city as soon as possible. Mom married my dad, a comic book illustrator, and Uncle Ray married my Uncle Charlie, a comic book writer, and together we all live a happy nerdy life in Cypress, a suburban pit stop of a town just outside of Houston. When you want to make something of your life, you move out of Pine Grove.

When you're miserable and alone, you go back.

Granny's house is a ranch-style white brick home with dark green trim and a big, welcoming front porch that's covered in potted plants. She lives at the end of a long, winding road, where every home has a bit of land

and plenty of room to throw loud parties without annoying the neighbors. I love it here, inside Granny's property. The rest of the town is nothing special, but here I can tuck away from everything back home. This house feels like a warm hug, filled with memories of summers spent reading books with Granny, and taking painting classes with her at the community center, giggling in the back row because she'd go wildly off script and paint a zebra in the middle of our mountain landscape.

When my friends meet Granny, they have to wipe their minds of all expectations about someone who is called *Granny*. Nina and I are the only people who even call her that, as I am the only grandchild and Nina is basically a surrogate granddaughter. To everyone else, she's Dot—short for Dorothy. She's not some old stereotypical matriarch with short gray hair, hunched over knitting needles. She's a white woman in her sixties, tall, blonde, and beautifully botoxed. Retired librarian, lifelong badass. She's the high-tech rocket ship of grandmas.

Granny swings the front door open, brandishing us with a red-lipped smile. "My babies are here."

Nina and I are immediately pulled into her orbit, squeezed into a long hug. Granny steps back slowly, one hand on each of our shoulders. "You're both getting so big. So grown up." A twinkle flashes in her bright blue eyes. "I wish Joe were here to see you." She bops me on the nose. "He'd be so proud."

The house smells like coconuts because Granny always matches her candles to the season, and that subtle spicy scent that always reminds me of home. Nina and I head down the long hallway to the room at the very end to drop off our bags. My mom's childhood bedroom is half guest room, half sewing room, containing only small hints of the person who used to live here. Mom's old

Zombie Radio poster is still thumbtacked into the wall next to a ripped out magazine page of Ashlee Simpson that's taped next to it. Mom's eclectic music tastes never stop surprising me. Even now, you can always find Billy Idol next to Zombie Radio next to Justin Bieber on her music playlists.

"You're doing it again," Nina says. She's standing on the other side of the bed, pulling her phone charger out from the zippered pocket on her bag. She leans over and plugs it into the wall. "Don't keep all those thoughts to yourself. Let 'em out."

"If I say everything I'm thinking, it'll drive you crazy," I say, sliding my hands over my hips, realizing too late that my leggings only have one side pocket and I can't hide my hands in there. I gaze around Mom's old bedroom, the place I've crashed every time I've stayed here, wishing the familiar nostalgia would push away the pain in my chest.

I'm sixty-seven miles away from Jonah. Why am I still thinking of him?

In the living room, Granny has set out a decorative tray on the coffee table. It has a pitcher of sweet tea, three cups, and a small charcuterie board. Nina plops to the floor and grabs a handful of green olives.

Granny pats the couch next to her. "Take a seat and tell me what ruined your summer."

I'd prefer not to speak of any of this, because I like to think I can make my problems go away by avoiding them completely. But my family is the kind of close that won't let you run from your problems.

I sit next to Granny and buy some time by pouring myself a cup of tea. Then, because she's going to find out anyway, I tell her.

"Addyson Deblois."

Granny's brow furrows. "I thought she was your

friend?"

Tears flood my eyes. Nina holds out a chocolate covered pretzel, a sugary offering to make me feel better. While I eat it, she says, "Addyson used her city council daddy to steal Emma's summer internship away from her."

Granny stiffens. "The observatory gig?"

I nod, breathing deeply through my nose to stop the tears. This pretzel tastes like cardboard. Broken hearts must mess with the wiring to your tongue because they make everything taste bad.

"What a little shit," Granny hisses, tucking a stray bit of hair behind her ear. Even when she's cursing, she looks prim and proper doing it. Her shoulders are back, and she sits tall, shaking her head. "I have never been a fan of that family."

The Deblois family are Pine Grove transplants as well. Addy became friends with Nina and me in sixth grade when we all had P.E. together. When Uncle Ray discovered her dad was city council member Donovan Deblois, he grimaced and told me not to trust her as far as I could throw her. I figured he just didn't like the councilman's policies or something, but he was right.

Despite volunteering at the Starr Observatory every summer since I was thirteen, I discovered Addy had been offered the job the same day I found out she'd stolen my boyfriend.

"It is what it is," I say, staring at my phone in my hand. Even though Jonah and I have been broken up for an entire five days, I can't stop the habit of checking my messages, expecting to see his name on my home screen, half a dozen heart emojis surrounding the name Jonah.

The only emoji next to his name now is the poop emoji.

Also, he hasn't texted me.

"There will be more summers," Granny says, patting my leg. "And if that girl is half as incompetent as her father, she'll probably get fired soon and they'll be begging you to take over."

"That's not all," Nina says, her dark eyes prodding me to reveal the other half of my broken heart to my grandmother.

"Oh?"

"Mom didn't tell you?" I ask.

She shakes her head. "What happened, honey?"

I look away, my eyes fixing on the massive flat screen TV on the wall. Many of my friends keep their personal lives a secret from family, but my family is always all up in my business. It's just how they are. And if I don't tell her now, Mom or Uncle Ray will soon enough.

I sigh. "Jonah left me for Addyson. And she got my dream summer internship. She's basically taken over my life."

"What a little shit," Granny says again, punctuating each word, her jaw tightening. "Emma, I am so sorry. What can I do? Let's do something. Do people still T-P houses? We could T-P her house."

The idea of my sixty-five year old grandmother laughing manically in the dark, running around Addy's massive McMansion and tossing rolls of toilet paper over the ornate landscaping is almost funny enough to break through my tears and make me smile.

"She needs a good scream," Nina says, stabbing a toothpick into a cube of cheddar. "Screaming will clear her lungs of all this bad energy."

"The barn would be a perfect place for that," Granny says. "It's well insulated. No one calls the cops out here, so you'll be free to scream all you want."

"Perfect!" Nina pushes up from the floor,

reaching for another handful of snacks. "Let's go."

The barn is a tan metal building with a concrete floor, a small loft, and lots and lots of junk. I never met my grandfather since he died shortly after I was born, but he was something of a mechanical hoarder. Two ancient tractors sit rusting in the main area of the barn, but the walls are lined with shelves of old sewing machines, engines, parts of motorcycles, and other random mechanical junk that would probably be an antique lover's dream.

The barn door closes with a rattle, kicking up dust that sparkles like microscopic stars in the glow of the skylight beaming down on us.

"All right." Nina cracks her knuckles, squatting down a bit like a wrestler preparing to tussle. "Let's do this."

"Are we seriously going to scream in a barn?"

She looks me right in the eyes, her expression devoid of any sarcasm. "Yes."

"What, like this?" I take a deep breath, toss my head back, and let out a yell.

"No!" she yells back, putting her hands on her hips. "That's pathetic. Do it again."

I scream again, this time tightening my fists at my sides.

Nina tsks, shaking her head. I get the distinct impression that this is also how she paces around when she coaches little kid soccer teams in the fall.

"That's not the scream of a broken heart—wait, give me that," she says, snatching the phone from my hand. I didn't even realize I was still holding it, unconsciously checking for texts every few minutes. She places it on a wooden table next to an ancient telescope I've never seen before. "Now yell like your heart is actually broken, you rebel scum!"

I quirk an eyebrow and she shrugs. "All that Star Wars stuff in your motel has worn off on me."

I take a deep breath, close my eyes, toss my head back, and scream. This time my voice isn't sharp and dainty—it's an anguished roar. Nina cheers me on, and I yell again, turning in a circle to get all this sad, broken energy out. My voice reverberates across the junk, like a disco ball of sound waves flooding every inch of the barn.

I don't know if it's helping mend all the pain in my heart, but I do know that it's fun.

"Oh, shit." Nina grabs my wrist. "Emma!"

"What?" I say, dizzy from yelling. I open my eyes.

"Your phone is on fire."

Chapter Two

It's not fire. It's smoke.

A bright pink smoke rises off my phone. Pink, like a new star formation in the galaxy, emitting a gorgeous cotton-candy hue, rising in a thin line that curls up into the air. My body warms as I approach it. A concentrated beam of light hits my phone screen, shooting out from the telescope's eyepiece, which is hovering right over the antique wooden table where Nina had placed my phone.

I reach out, mesmerized.

"Emma, don't!" Nina says, but she's not close enough to see what I see.

My phone is perfectly fine. I pick it up, turn it over, and click on the screen, blinking in surprise when I see a photo of my mom. She thought she was funny when she changed out my lock screen image to be a goofy picture of her, wearing her dark rimmed glasses and sticking out her tongue, instead of what it used to be, a picture of Jonah and me. His arms wrapped around my shoulders. His lips pressed to my cheek. My eyes, sparkling with the high of being in love.

I turn off the screen.

"What the hell was that?" Nina looks around as if intimating the empty air to do it again. But everything is quiet and perfectly normal.

"I don't know." I shove my phone in my pocket and peer down at the telescope. All evidence of the pink smoke has vanished—only floating bits of dust and bright summer sunlight beams across the cluttered room from the skylights above.

"That was weird."

"Yeah." I nod, peering at the device in front of

me. "This telescope is dope."

It's old. Definitely antique. It's thin and narrow, made of a goldish metal. Brass, maybe. It's about three feet long and sits on an attached dainty metal tripod. I've never seen it before, but I also never explore the barn. Over the years, I've only come in here a few times to help Granny transport her plastic bins of holiday decorations before and after each season.

Leaning over, I lift the eye piece and peer through it. The cap on the other side is off, hanging from a brass chain, but peering through the telescope shows me nothing but black darkness. I tilt it up toward the skylight, but still can't see anything.

"Must be broken."

The barn door rattles open. "I don't hear yelling," Granny sing-songs, shoving the door open wider with her hip. She's carrying the charcuterie board. The green olives have been refilled after Nina decimated them. "I bought a ton of food for the summer, so I can't let it go to waste. Plus all that yelling should give you an appetite."

"I love being here," Nina says, dunking a piece of cheese in jalapeno marmalade before popping it in her mouth.

All I've had to eat all day is the chocolate milkshake we got at the start of our two-hour road trip and one single pretzel, but I'm not hungry. Curiosity burns in my belly instead.

"Granny, where did this telescope come from?"

"Same place all this other crap came from," she says, glancing around. "Joe found it at the flea market. He loved gazing out at the stars."

"Just like Emma," Nina says. She stacks cheese and slices of pepperoni between two crackers and bites down on it, not caring about the crumbs that land on her shirt.

"Just like Emma," Granny repeats, reaching over and squeezing my upper arm. I notice her eyes dip to my necklace, a white gold pendant of my star sign, Taurus, made with small diamonds connected to look like the constellation. It looks like a sideways stick figure that's missing a head. Granny got it for my sixteenth birthday.

"Well, it's broken now," I say, poking at the eyepiece that almost ruined my phone a moment ago.

"It's always been broken," Granny says with a chuckle. "The sign on it at the flea market said it was broken."

"So why is it set up like it's ready to look at the sky?" I ask. Of all the haphazardly stashed junk in this barn, the telescope looks like it was placed right here under the skylight on purpose.

She shrugs. "Who knows why your grandfather did the things he did."

"Okay." Nina claps her hands together in front of her chest. "All three of us—one big final scream—and then we will have successfully started our summer off right."

Granny holds out her hands to us, and we form a triangle in the center of the barn. She counts down from three, and then we all yell at the top of our lungs. I can't help myself. I belt out exactly what I'm thinking.

"I hate you, Jonah Pena!"

Granny and Nina look at each other, eyes wide, before turning to me.

"That's it," I say with a shrug. "That was the scream that cured me."

Laughter fills the barn, and although it only lasts a second, it's true. For one tiny little moment, I am cured of this heartache. I am happy. I am whole.

Then a few seconds later the pain jolts back, cracking open my chest again. Maybe it'll take more than one evening at Granny's house to mend my broken heart, but that's okay. I'm here for the summer.

****

"We should do something for Granny," I say, hours later when Nina and I are crawling into the guest bed in my mom's old bedroom. It's almost midnight, which is early on the scale of summer vacation bedtimes, but I haven't slept since Jonah dumped me, and the drive was long, and screaming at the top of your lungs for an hour will drain you.

"Like what?" she says, digging deodorant out of her backpack and slopping it under her arms. Her hair is still damp from her shower and she smells like crisp, summer days and cute boys.

She bought shampoo from the men's section of Alan's Grocery where we'd stocked up on essentials after scarfing down Granny's chicken enchiladas for dinner. It's a good-smelling shampoo, but it reminds me too much of Jonah. He always had that same chemically manufactured boy smell from using products like those.

From freshman year until just one week ago, I thought boy smell was the greatest smell ever, followed by coffee, and a freshly laundered basket of motel linens, still warm from the dryer. I spent three years leaning into Jonah, snuggling against his collarbone, breathing in that artificial woodsy, mountain air scent that clung to his skin. When we'd first started dating, he loaned me his hoodie, and I'm embarrassed to admit I slept with that thing for two weeks, my heart fluttering every time I inhaled the scent of him.

It smells better on Nina.

When I had decided to stay here in Pine Grove for the summer, I imagined nights spent cuddled up with a pint of ice cream and sad movies, and my sad music playlist, and sad walks around the town's only park. But now Nina is here and Granny seems thrilled for our company, and the summer feels like it's just bursting with potential.

I consider my suggestion, trying to think of a nice thing to do for the woman who has everything she wants. "Donuts," I say, snapping my fingers. "We should get up early and sneak out and grab a dozen donuts from that place she loves."

"The square donut place?" Nina says. *"Yes."*

Pine Grove doesn't have chain stores like we do in the city. Its one and only donut shop is family owned, and their donuts are squares with circle holes in the middle. I don't know why they chose to break the circular donut tradition, but they're delicious and Granny loves them. When I was a kid and would spend weekends with her, she'd always take me to get a square donut before dropping me off back at home.

"We'll have to get up early. Like *early*, early." I reach for my phone and open the clock app. "Granny is usually up by 7:00, so we should get up at 6:00."

"Okay, but only because Granny Dot is the coolest grandma on the planet." Nina says, yawning as she crawls into bed. "I only wake up early for cool grannies and track meets and that's it."

I snort and set my phone's alarm for 6:00 in the morning. With the lamp off, the room blooms into darkness, save for the little pink and green plastic stars stuck to the ceiling. Mom said she'd put them up there when she was a teenager, and they're still here all these years later.

"Emma?" Nina whispers beside me in the bed.

"Yes?" I whisper back.

She rolls over. In the darkness, I picture her facing me, but all I see is a blurry lump against the backdrop of the window behind her. "Does your heart feel any better?"

Her voice is so hopeful that I'll say yes. A twinge of guilt tugs at the back of my throat. I could lie to make her feel better. If it were anyone else, I probably would lie. But there's no point in bending the truth with your best friend. I love her too much to treat her like a fool.

I take a shuddering breath. My mind shows me pictures of Jonah, even though I don't want it to. The worst part is that my subconscious only reminds me of the good times. The happy times. Not the day he broke my heart. Not the guilty, awful way he looked as he told me he didn't want to be my boyfriend anymore.

I exhale. "Not really."

"Maybe tomorrow."

"Yeah," I say, peering at the dozens of plastic stars above me, an imaginary galaxy leading to nowhere. "Maybe tomorrow."

I don't know when I drift off to sleep, but the piercing lullaby of my phone alarm wakes me up exactly at 6:00 in the morning. With my eyes closed, I reach over, feeling for my phone. I knock something else to the floor instead. Weird. There's nothing on this nightstand except my phone and the lamp.

I blink awake, yawning in the early morning hour. My fingers finally wrap around my phone. I shut off the alarm and sit up in bed.

Nina must already be up. She even made her half of the bed while I was still sleeping. That's not like her. If it were up to Nina, bed-making would be illegal. Maybe she just really wants to impress Granny by being a super polite house guest. Maybe she snuck out even earlier to get the donuts so I can sleep in later. Seems like something she would do.

I fall back, pulling the sheets back up to my chin and closing my eyes to get a few more minutes of sleep—

only these aren't the sheets I fell asleep in. These are a black jersey cotton material, not pink floral. Maybe I'm mistaken. Granny likes to keep things clean, but there's no way she'd change the sheets in the middle of the night while we're sleeping on them. I must be mistaken.

And I must be extremely mistaken again when I look around the room and see a collection of clothes, two guitars, and dozens of vintage posters all over the place like some kind of thrift store threw up in here. This isn't Granny's sewing stuff. The Zombie Radio and Ashlee Simpson posters are still there, so I haven't gone completely insane.

Just ... mostly insane?

My heartbeat pounds in my ears. Everything goes a little blurry. This is a dream, I realize. A dream. Shoving my fists into my eyes does nothing to wake me up. Neither does tugging my hair or pinching my arm. This strange room stays exactly how it is, filled with random crap that wasn't here before. I sit up, chest heaving as panic threatens to consume me.

A male voice starts singing in the hallway, some made up song about getting knocked down then getting back up again and pissing the night away. The off-key singer almost sounds like Uncle Ray, only different.

When the figure in the hallway walks past the door, he stops, surprise painting over his brown skin. Dark curly hair pokes out on all sides of his head. He's holding a massive device that looks like a hair straightener. Seriously, the metal plates are the size of my palm.

He even looks like Uncle Ray. Only ... not.

This man is a teenager. Does my uncle have some secret teenage son I don't know about? Who is living at Granny's house ... and no one told me...?

"Who are you?" he asks curiously, leaning against

the door frame. I barely hear him over the thundering of my heartbeat in my ears. "Did Lindsey bring you home? I thought she wasn't coming back for a couple more days."

Lindsey? My mom.

My gaze wanders to a Star Wars calendar that's nailed next to the door. It has the old movie characters, not the new ones. But it's not a young Harrison Ford dressed as Han Solo that makes my blood turn to ice. It's the date, printed at the top of the month of June in black Star Wars font.

2004.

Chapter Three

"Uncle Ray?" My voice is soft and high and not at all my voice. It's the voice of someone else, some other person having one hell of a hallucination.

Ray—because I know it's Ray, it has to be—takes one step into the room, eyes narrowed. His brown skin is smooth and youthful, missing those thin lines across his forehead and the laugh lines in his cheeks. His hair is long and curly, the way I remember from my childhood, not like the trimmed look he wears now. And he's chubby, with rounder cheeks and a slight gut. But it's him.

"Uncle?" he says. "I'm not an uncle. Wait, is that some kind of new slang or something?"

"Ray," I clarify, gripping the black sheets in my fists. "You're Ray Ross?"

"Yes…" He scans the room. "Uncle is fine with me, I guess. It's better than dawg." He rolls his eyes. The cord of the hair straightener scrapes across the wooden floor. "I am so sick of dawg. I blame MTV. It's just not as good as it used to be, ya know?"

I hear all his words, but I don't process them over the sound of my raging heartbeat as the organ tries to escape my chest.

"Granny?" I call out, looking past him and into the hallway. I still haven't stood up from the bed, but I'm not sure I'm even capable of moving right now. "Nina!"

Ray quirks an eyebrow. "No one with those names live here. Are you in the right house? Where's Lindsey?"

The mother of all panic attacks slides into the room, wraps around me, and dives straight into my throat, tentacles of panic and fear wrapping around my lungs and spreading out into my bones. Panic is practically a tangible monster in the room. This can't possibly be happening. *Get it together, Emma.*

I try to swallow but my mouth is dry. "What year is it?"

"Exactly how many pots have you smoked?" he snorts, like he's just said something funny.

Tears pour down my cheeks. I push out of the bed on shaky limbs and walk over to the calendar. "Is it really 2004?"

"Uh, yes," my too-young uncle says sarcastically. "Same year it was yesterday. Same year it'll be tomorrow. Seriously, are you on drugs? I can get you some help, or water, or something."

"I'm not on drugs." I shake my head, trying to shuffle around all my thoughts, make them settle down into some order that makes sense. At least, I don't think I'm on drugs. Maybe there's been a gas leak and I'm slowly dying and my brain is conjuring up this weird dream in my last few moments alive.

I shudder at the fear of dying without even knowing I'm dying. I pinch myself again. *Wake up. Wake up!*

My eyes smash closed and I try to breathe. I try to inhale. Exhale. Inhale. Like a person who is living their life the way they're supposed to. Like the person I was last night.

After a few steady breaths, I open my eyes again, hoping to see the world put back the way it should be. Instead, I see the younger version of my uncle watching me with furrowed brows and a pitying look.

"I'm not on drugs," I say again. "I don't even drink."

"So … what's wrong?" he asks.

I swallow.

He's going to think I'm crazy.

"It's the year 2024."

"No … it's 2004."

My entire body trembles in fear and confusion. A little bit of anger is swelling up in me, too. This is a cruel joke. It has to be. "It's June, 2024. When I went to bed last night it was June, 2024."

"Cool," he says with a dismissive nod, switching the hair straightener to his other hand. "So, you're a time traveler? Very cool."

"Why are you being so sarcastic?" I put a hand to my chest, willing my heart to slow down. This much tachycardia is going to kill me. A bead of sweat rolls down my back.

"Is this real? Is this actually happening?" My breath is ragged. My heart thuds. My vision is going blurry around the edges. Suddenly all I want is a small bit of reassurance. A hug. A smile. Nina.

"I need you to believe me," I say as tears pour out of my eyes. "Please believe me. I don't know what's going on."

"Oh sure, yeah, I believe you."

The tone of his voice says he in fact does not believe me. He smirks, eyes dropping down my chest.

"Your shirt says Cypress High Class of 2025. That's twenty-one years from now. Anyone who graduates in twenty-one years hasn't been born yet, so clearly you're…" he wiggles his fingers and lowers his voice, "from the fuuuu-ture."

The only reply I can muster is a panicked sob.

He snaps his fingers. "This is a joke. I'm being set up."

He peers around the room suspiciously, then bolts over to the closet, yanking open the door revealing—nothing. Just tons of clothes, half hung up and half on the floor. "Lindsey," he calls out. "Very funny. Excellent prank. Now get out here and do my hair. You're the only one who can get the parts in the back good enough."

This is not happening. This is so not happening. And yet … seconds pass with my teenage uncle wandering around trying to find someone who isn't in the room.

"You have to believe me, Uncle Ray. You're one of my best friends. In my world I can trust you with anything. Please."

Digging through the sheets, I retrieve my phone.

"That is a fancy camera," he says, stopping in his tracks. "It's so flat."

"It's my phone."

His eyes widen. That smug smirk slides right off his face.

"I can prove I'm from the future." I tap my photo gallery and pull up a recent picture of Uncle Ray, taken a few weeks ago when we got a custom set of Portal mirrors for the motel, complete with orange and blue LED lights around the edges to make it look like the real thing. In the photo, he's standing in front of the orange one, pretending to fall into the portal.

"This is you," I say, turning the phone to him.

His jaw drops as he peers at the screen. I swipe to the next photo, which features the two of us acting goofy in front of the blue portal mirror. "That's me and that's you," I say, holding out the phone. He flinches as if my iPhone will bite him. I hold it closer. "There's me, looking normal like I do now, and you—only you're older because it was taken in my time. In 2024 when you're thirty-eight."

He's quiet for a long moment, studying the photo. He puts a hand on his stomach pooch. "Damn, I look fit."

"It's not an aging filter, I swear. It's real."

"Aging filter?"

"Yeah, like from Snapchat."

"Snapchat?"

"It's an app," I say, realizing a little too late that someone from his time has no idea what Snapchat is. "It's … a social media thing."

"Don't tell me," he says, standing up. He paces the length of the room then turns back around, dragging his hands over his face. "Don't tell me anything from your time. I can't know anything."

A tiny spark of relief warms up the center of my chest. "Does this mean you believe me?"

"If I'm your uncle, does that mean Lindsey is your mom?"

"Yes."

His eyes widen and he turns around, palms pressed to his forehead. He looks like one of those guys on a talk show who just found the *DNA confirmed they are the father*. He exhales loudly, then looks at me.

"You're white, so that fits, but you don't really look like her."

"I look more like my dad." It's a crime, really, how I take after his stocky frame with dark boring hair that won't hold a curl and dingy, dark brown eyes. Mom is lovely, with auburn hair and Irish green eyes, and let's be honest, totally out of Dad's league.

He peers at me. "Where did you come from?"

"I'm visiting my granny for the summer, and I went to bed last night in this room. Only it's not Mom's room in my time, it's the guest room. And my best friend Nina was with me,

and—" I toss my arms up. "I woke up this morning to this."

"Whoa," he says, exhaling.

"So you believe me, right?"

"Yeah… I … I guess I do."

"Thank you." More tears pour from my eyes and I grab him, squeezing him hard to me. "Thank you, thank you, thank you."

Teenage Uncle Ray is chubbier than modern day Uncle Ray, but he smells the same. Like shea butter and freshly cut lumber.

"How did this even happen?" His voice is strained against the death grip of my hug.

I pull back. "I don't know."

"This house must have a … a … portal. A wormhole…" He drops down, peering under the bed. When he sits up, his eyes are alight with wonder. "We need to get you back home."

"Yes," I say with an eager nod. "Yes, we do. How do we do that?"

"I don't know. There are tons of time travel theories … sci-fi novels, movies … any number of them could have it right. Or maybe they're all wrong." I can see the wheels in his mind churning, just like they do when he's coming up with the perfect cosplay for our yearly trip to Comicpalooza. Uncle Ray is smart. He'll figure this out. He will get me home.

"It's a good thing Lindsey isn't here," he says, pacing around the room, teeth digging into his thumbnail. "She can't see you. No one else can know who you are, okay? Don't tell me anything. Just one tiny change in the timeline can be catastrophic."

"Where is my mom?"

"She's traveling around with her friends, following her favorite band's summer tour schedule. Well, to all the places she can afford to drive to."

"Oh, right. The summer Zombie Radio tour. She talks about that epic summer all the time."

"Don't tell me!" He covers his hands over his

ears. "I can't know this."

"Sorry."

"Okay." He holds out his hands. "We have to get you back to your timeline. But we don't know how to do that yet, and I have to go to work soon. I can't just *not* go because that's changing the timeline. I have to do everything exactly as normal."

"I'll stay here."

"No way. Dad already went to work, but my mom is home. She'll wake up soon and see you and interact with you." He shakes his head. "No, that's not safe. You'll come to work with me, and you'll just sit in the back out of sight. I'm the only person who works on weekdays, so we should be fine."

"And then what do I do? Sleep in the woods?"

"You'll sleep in my room. We'll say you're my new girlfriend or something, and say you feel sick or something, so you have to stay in my room. My parents are cool. No one will mess with you."

"Why would they believe that?" I ask.

He shrugs. "Just act sick. Or we could say someone in your family just died and you're really sad about it so you don't want to talk to anyone."

"No, I mean, the girlfriend thing?"

He goes completely still. "Why wouldn't they believe that?"

I feel like I'm being tested and every answer I give will be the wrong one.

"Because…" My teeth dig into my lip. "You're … gay?"

"In the future?" his voice is a whisper.

I nod.

"No," he says, shaking his head and waving his hands. "No, no, no. Don't answer. Don't say anything about the future."

"My lips are sealed."

"Good." He grabs the hair straightener. "I have to get ready. Come hang out in my room. And if anyone asks, you're my sick girlfriend."

"Okay."

He rushes into the hallway. I swear I see just a hint of a smile on his otherwise shell-shocked face.

Chapter Four

My Uncle Ray is a straight up scene kid. I can't stop staring at his wavy black hair, now flat-ironed straight across his eyes, which are now rimmed in black eyeliner. He wears a black T-shirt with the Magic Mark's Pizza logo on it, paired with dark blue Dickie's work pants and red Converse. I'm still wearing the shirt and leggings I slept in, plus a borrowed pair of Mom's black and white checkered Vans slip-ons. She still has these shoes, or a pair that looks just like them in 2024. I guess some things never go out of style.

"What?" Ray says, glancing at me while he drives us to the pizza place where he works.

"Nothing."

I run my hand over the smooth gray dashboard in front of me. Uncle Ray's white 1998 Ford Mustang is something of a legend in my time. He loves this car. There's a framed photo of it hanging in his living room back at our motel. My grandfather won it in a charity raffle when it was brand new, and after driving it for a few years, he gave it to Ray.

I admire the car on the short drive, and I do not tell him its future fate. Flooded by Hurricane Katrina.

"How are you holding up?" he asks.

"I'm scared shitless."

"Me, too."

"But it's also kind of amazing," I say, flipping through the massive CD book I found on the floorboard. "I mean, *what* is happening? *How* is this happening?"

He blows out air through his nose. "Hell if I know. I wish I could ask you so many things, but I can't."

"You could," I say, peering at a homemade CD with *Ray's summer jams* written in Sharpie. "I doubt it would hurt anything if you're the only person who knew."

"No. Absolutely not. If I've learned anything from a lifetime of reading science fiction, it's that you can't mess up the timeline. The best thing we can do is get you back to 2024 as soon as possible. But first, I have to finish my shift."

Magic Mark's Pizza doesn't exist in my time, but the shopping center does. It's the only big retail space in Pine Grove. Nina and I were just at Alan's Grocery last night, which is still here to the right of the long strip of connected stores, but with an older plastic sign instead of the modern façade it has now.

I get out of his car and gaze up at the red and green pizza sign. There's an attorney's office to the left of the pizza place, followed by a nail salon, a Radio Shack, and some place called Sam's Music. To the right is T&T Vacuum Repair, then Alan's Grocery. Besides Alan's, none of these businesses still exist in my time. The parking lot is the same. The sky above looks the same. The warm summer air feels the same.

But nothing is the same.

"Weird."

"Huh?" Ray calls out, glancing over his shoulder at me as he unlocks the store's front door.

"Nothing."

Inside, he pulls the cord on the neon OPEN sign, flips on the cash register, then reaches behind the red and green counter and tosses a T-shirt to me. It looks brand new but smells like pizza. "Go to the bathroom and put this on," he says. "That Class of 2025 shirt is creepy."

Magic Mark's has a salad bar, a soda fountain with the Pepsi logo on it, and a small dine-in area of green tables and red chairs. It looks a lot like the eateries at home, and the general sameness of everything gives me the first ounce of comfort I've had in the hour that I've been awake this morning. The lump in my throat lessens a little. Every few minutes I still get a random burst of adrenaline, a mini panic attack that seizes my insides and makes me want to run. But where would I run to?

The road we took to drive here has only two lanes right now. In my world, it has four, plus a turning lane in the middle. And red lights at the intersections instead of "stop" signs. While Pine Grove is a small town in my time, it's even smaller now.

Instinctively, I reach for the pocket on my thigh, but it's empty.

My uncle had declared my phone a "terrifying future doohickey" and made me hide it in his bedroom so no one would find it and realize it's from the future. It didn't get any service anyway, but I still feel naked without it. My shoulders fall. "I miss my phone."

"Who are you going to call?" Ray says with a snort as he refills the buckets of pizza toppings with fresh bags from the walk-in fridge.

"I don't really use my phone for calling."

"Oh, right. It's also a digital camera."

Behind us, the industrial oven beeps, signaling that it's preheated and ready for pizzas. Ray moves to a stack of pre-cut cardboard and starts folding them into pizza boxes. I pick one up and fold it, taking ten times as long as him to figure out exactly how to bend each piece into the correct shape.

Despite me asking multiple times, Ray won't let me make a pizza. I guess he's too scared that I'll find a way to mess up the timeline by tossing some cheese, peppers, and black olives onto a pizza crust. I hang around in the kitchen and watch him make, cut, and box pizzas. When customers come inside to pick up their food, I have to stay hidden in the back. Ray seems to think the simple act of a random customer seeing me might mess up the timeline.

The secrecy reminds me of the time Jonah accidentally fell asleep while watching a movie at my house. We were just cuddled up on the couch—totally innocent—but when we woke up in the morning, Jonah panicked, worried my parents would freak if they found out. My mom and dad are on the cooler end of the parent spectrum, but we were sixteen and not in the mood for a spontaneous "dangers of getting knocked up as a teen" talk. I'd made him stay in my room for hours until my parents finally went downstairs to the motel lobby and I could sneak him out through a fire escape.

Those were the good old days of our relationship. When we were young and stupidly in love, before he decided he'd make a great mayor one day and started volunteering for Mr. Donny Deblois's city council reelection campaign. We didn't know it back then, but last summer was the last summer we'd be a couple. Shortly after, he started crushing on Donny's daughter, Addyson.

He swears he didn't cheat on me, but all those late nights spent at Donny's house doing quote-quote *campaign stuff* makes that a little sus, if you ask me.

My teeth grind together.

I loved Jonah.

I mean, I thought I did. Maybe I didn't. Maybe my love for Jonah was a cubic zirconia—fashioned in a lab instead of a true mined diamond, taken out of the depths of the earth.

Maybe I'm too young and foolish to know real love.

But my love of space is absolutely, one hundred percent the real deal. My fascination with the universe, the very fabric of our own existence as told in the stars—that's rock hard diamond love.

That summer internship at the observatory should have been mine. I've volunteered there for years. I know all four employees by name. I even wrote a stellar cover letter, complete with two references from both my astronomy and AP Chem teachers, explaining in detail how smart and amazing I am. My interview went perfectly. I was told I'd hear back about my internship schedule in the next few days. I then talked my parents into hiring a temporary summer employee to cover for me at the motel, and I asked Granny if I could stay with her for the summer since she lives near the observatory.

The internship was mine.

But Addy stole it, too.

I take a deep breath, holding the air in my lungs until they feel like they're going to explode.

"You're ridiculous," I mutter to myself as I spin around in the office chair. "You've magically time traveled back twenty years into the past and you're still wallowing in self-pity. Way to go, Emma."

Hours pass. If this were any other day, I'd be bored out of my mind being stuck here in the small office at the back of the pizza shop, but my mind is running a mile a minute, which keeps me occupied. After hiding away for the busy lunch hour, I get up and peer around the corner into the front of the restaurant.

Uncle Ray leans on the counter, the corded work phone tucked under his hair. He doodles on the order pad while talking on the phone in a voice too quiet for me to hear. Must be a personal call.

A short while later, he drops the phone into the receiver and drums his hands on the countertop. "Hey, Emma?"

"Yeah?" I say, stepping out from the back. He

doesn't look like he's just discovered how to build a time machine so I can go home, but hope still digs at my chest anyway.

"I'm gonna run to Sam's real quick."

"Who's Sam?"

"It's the music store," he says, nodding his head toward the end of the shopping center. "I'll be back in a couple minutes. Just ignore the phone if it rings."

He's out the door before I can reply, the jingle of bells clacking against the glass behind him. I slip back into the office.

"Hello?" a feminine voice calls out a few minutes later.

I freeze. Seconds drip on and on, and there's no Uncle Ray in sight.

"Hello?" the voice calls out again. "Anyone alive in here?"

I step out from the back. "Sorry," I say, tugging at my new T-shirt that makes me look like an actual employee. I glance out the window, hoping to see Ray walking back, but the sidewalk is empty. "How can I help you?"

"Pickup for Marci," she says, glancing at the phone in her hand. It's a pink flip phone, the kind of vintage thing I've only seen in old movies, but never in real life. She looks like she's in her early twenties, wearing flared bottom blue jeans and a pink lacy halter top that shows off her pink sparkly belly button ring. Her pale skin looks dry under a layer of powdery makeup, and her light blonde hair is pulled back with a rhinestone headband. Her shoes are three inches tall, made of black foam, and have even more tacky rhinestones along the straps. She's incredible.

"One second," I say, slipping into the safety of the kitchen area. Sure enough, a freshly baked pizza hangs out at the end of the oven's conveyer belt, waiting patiently to be cut into slices and boxed. Crap. Why did Ray have to leave when someone's order was almost ready?

"It's almost ready," I call out. I reach for the oddly-shaped pliers and grab the pizza pan out of the oven just like I've seen Ray do a dozen times this morning. The pizza slides easily out onto the cutting board. The pizza slices may not come out exactly even, but at least I figure out how to get it sliced and slid into the box without ruining the thing. I fold the lid and carry the pizza out to the front of the restaurant.

She puts a twenty-dollar bill on the counter. Only there's no possible way I can figure out how to do this. What does a pizza cost in 2004? The register is covered in buttons with abbreviations written in pen on little white stickers. Half the stickers are rubbed off from use.

Our register at the motel is a freaking iPad with a touchless credit card base. I don't know how to work this thing!

"Your pizza is free today," I say, giving her my best customer service smile as I slide the twenty dollar bill back to her.

"Really? Why?"

I shrug. "I'm new here and no one taught me how to work the register."

"Awesome sauce." She shoves the money into the dainty pink handbag that hangs from her arm. I get a sudden and unexpected mental picture of Cher from the movie Clueless.

Her phone beeps and she flips it back open with her thumb, lips pressing into a flat line as she looks at the screen. "O-M-G I freaking hate you," she tells the phone. "Sorry," she says, smiling up at me. "Ignore me. I'm having boyfriend issues."

41

"I know the feeling all too well," I say.

She snaps the phone closed. "It's just like, every other day my boyfriend ditches me for his stupid friends. Like, literally every other day, ever since he got a camcorder for Christmas. We'll have plans to do something and then he's like, *nah never mind, I'd rather see my dumbass bros and do dumbass bro shit like Bam Margera.* He's never going to get famous. I mean, he *is* a jackass, but not like, a Jackass, jackass, ya know?"

I do not in fact know, but I nod and let her talk.

She shakes her head. "I don't know why I put up with him."

"So don't," I say. "If he wants to choose his friends over you, then he can have his friends all the time. You deserve someone who won't ditch you."

"You're right." She nods quickly, pointing the stubby antenna end of her phone at me. "You're totally right. I do deserve better. Thanks, girlie."

"Yep," I say, wishing Ray would hurry up and get back before another customer comes in here and talks my ear off using lingo and references I don't understand. She waves goodbye and slips out the door, her free pizza in tow. Once she's gone, I rush over and turn the deadbolt, locking the door until Ray comes back five minutes later, a weird half-smile on his face.

"What took you so long?" I snap.

"It wasn't that long."

"You took like ten minutes."

"Sorry," he says, heading to the back. "Where's Marci's pizza?"

"I had to cut it up and give it to her," I say, leaning against the wall, arms crossed. I bet I look exactly like my mom right now, right down to the way her lips flatten in a disappointed frown when I've done something particularly annoying.

"Shit," he mutters, glancing out at the front of the store. "Did you say anything?"

"Yeah, I said *hi, my name is Emma Fitzgerald and I'm from the future, wanna know some fun facts you can use to get rich gambling on future events?*"

He rolls his eyes.

"I gave her the pizza for free because I didn't know how to work the register and you were taking forever to come back."

"Hopefully that doesn't ruin the timeline."

I shrug. "I don't see how it could."

Chapter Five

We come home to an empty house after Ray's shift is over, but he still sneaks me in as if I'm illegal contraband, shuffling me through the house and down the hall to his bedroom. I barely get to take in the sight of the tan carpet that's tile flooring in my time, the shelf of DVDs by the big, square television that doesn't exist anymore, and a worn blue recliner I've never seen before next to the old leather couches that still exist in Granny's house today. They look brand new now.

"Okay," Ray says, pressing his bedroom door closed, then sitting at the small white desk in his bedroom. "Now we figure out how to get you back home."

I walk around, taking in all the nerd stuff taped to his walls, the lightsaber on his dresser, and the most impressive CD collection I've ever seen. His bed is bunk beds, a white metal frame with the bottom bed bigger than the one up top. The bed frame is covered with music stickers, some of them band names I recognize, but most of them I don't.

"You haven't changed much," I say, touching a framed picture of my uncle from Comic Con when he got to meet Chewbacca. "You still have this."

"Don't tell me," he says, resignation tinging his voice. "Don't say anything, Emma. I'm serious. I can't know about the future."

I kneel down by his shelf that's filled with books and CDs and remove the paperback at the bottom left, taking my phone from where we'd stashed it this morning. I'm relieved to see it still here. This is probably the longest I've been without my phone since I first got a phone. I turn it on, smiling at the picture of Mom for half a second before my brain goes all backstabby and conjures up memories of Jonah's photo that used to be here.

"How the hell am I literally in another time and I'm still not over my ex?"

Muscle memory has me opening my texts, clicking on Jonah's name. Poop emoji Jonah left me the last four texts.

Jonah: **would you be happier if I had cheated?**

Jonah: **I mean seriously, Emma. I came clean and told you. I did the right thing.**

Emma: **Just last week you told me I had nothing to worry about, and now this? It's bullshit, Jonah, and you know it. I can't believe you did this to me.**

Jonah: **things change**

Emma: **I loved you.**

Jonah: **I'm sorry, but things changed.**

Pain clenches my chest. I've read this a hundred times. I have it memorized. And every time I read his last words to me, I can't help but scroll up a bit to the texts he used to send me, back when he was heart emoji Jonah.

Jonah: **love youuuuu**

Emma: **love youuuuu more**

Jonah: **gn baby**

Emma: **<3**

My eyes sting with tears as I scroll, and scroll, and scroll. Four years' worth of texts from my boyfriend. The Jonah who loved me as much as I loved him. We were supposed to be together forever. We were supposed to be that high school sweethearts story that our grandchildren told their grandchildren about.

And then Addyson Deblois stole him away from me.

"Emma?" Uncle Ray's voice slices through my

thoughts.

"Huh?" I look up. I'm still squatting on the floor by the bookshelf like some kind of Lord of the Rings troll. My phone is my *precious*, its memories and heartaches contained in the palm of my hand. To be honest, I love my phone on a regular day. But here in the past where every single thing is different makes my phone even more precious to me. This phone and the clothes I woke up in are all I have in this dated version of the planet.

"Are you even listening? I'm trying to figure out how to get you back home."

"Sorry." I sit on the foot of his bed, my teeth digging into my bottom lip. "How do we get me back home?"

"First we have to figure out why you're here. The most obvious reason someone time travels is because they invent a time machine and do it on purpose." He looks at me.

"I definitely didn't do that," I say when it's clear he expects an answer. "What's the next obvious reason someone time travels?"

He brushes his slick-straight black hair out of his eyes. "I don't know."

There's a sharp knock on his bedroom door and then it swings open, and I'm staring at a stunningly beautiful version of Granny. She wears black capris and a watermelon red tank top that shows off her tan and toned arms. A library ID hangs from a lanyard around her neck. Her big, billowy blonde hair is pulled into a high ponytail. The fine lines and wrinkles I know are gone, but her signature red lipstick looks just like I've always known.

"Oh!" she says, eyes wide. "I'm sorry. Didn't you know you had company, son."

"This is Emma." Ray swallows, his face a mix of anxiety and surprise that probably matches my own. "She's my—friend," he says, his cheeks a little pinker. Guess he chickened out about the whole fake girlfriend thing. I mean, yeah, it's weird.

Granny beams. "I figured you had someone new in your life," she says, winking at me. "You've seemed a little … extra happy lately."

The idea of my uncle and I in love is a little hilarious and also weird because he's family and also not into girls, and I have to bite down on my lip to keep from laughing.

"It's not like that," Ray says quickly. "She's having trouble at home, so I said she could crash here for a few days. Is that okay?"

"Sure thing," Granny says, turning her smile on me. "I take it that means you'll be here for dinner?"

"Um." I glance at Ray.

"Yeah," he says. "If that's okay."

She nods. "Always."

The moment Granny closes the door again, Ray and I turn to each other, eyes wide.

"Oh, my god," he says, scrubbing his hands down his face. "That is not how that was supposed to go. I didn't even hear them get home!"

"Them?"

"Mom and Dad."

"Oh. Right." Chills prickle across my arms. Ray's dad. Joe. The grandfather I've never met.

"What?" Ray says curiously, followed quickly by a shake of his head. "No. Don't tell me."

"Don't worry," I say. "I wasn't going to."

At the dining table, I can't stop staring at a fascinating piece of history—the family computer. I've seen old technology in movies, but you never realize just how big and boxy everything was back in this time. Even the keyboard seems bigger and uglier than the oldest keyboards forgotten in the back of my high school's computer lab. The monitor is square and boxy, the CPU an ugly gray. I have friends with gaming computers, but their CPUs are sleek and clear with colorful LED lights inside. This thing just looks ugly.

There is only one computer in this house, situated in a public corner of the kitchen, all out in the open so anyone can see what you're doing on it. It's so weird thinking about how my mom and uncle grew up like this. I have a phone more capable of anything this old hunk of junk can do, plus my own MacBook at home and then my school laptop, a Chromebook they issue to every student every year.

"I have three computers," I tell Uncle Ray when he walks in with two glasses of sweet tea.

He gives me a glass and sits next to me. Granny and Joe are outside on the back patio grilling dinner. I offered to help, but Ray gave me an anxious side-eye because he's afraid me helping cook dinner will somehow change all of the future as we know it, and then Granny said I'm their guest so I should just sit down and relax.

"That's not surprising. I imagine technology gets cheaper as time goes on," he says. "As soon as my parents go to sleep, we'll get online and Google time travel. See if we can find anything helpful. Oh, and *Google* means to like, search stuff online."

"Yeah, I know," I say with a snort.

"I guess Google sticks around in the future?"

"You have no idea how much it sticks around."

"Right," he says, taking a deep breath. I can tell he's just as curious to know about the future as I am desperate to tell him. But we both stay quiet out of respect for the time continuum.

The sliding glass door to the patio opens. I'm still not used to Granny being a certified bombshell in her forties. She's so beautiful it hurts. And here I am, the daughter of her adoptive daughter, sharing exactly zero DNA with the woman, which means I have no hope of ever looking like her.

"Dinner is served," she says, placing a platter of shrimp and veggie kebabs on the table. "Help yourself, everyone."

The man who walks through the patio door now, wearing khaki shorts, Converse, and a black Metallica t-shirt, is taller than I'd imagined. He's got to be over six feet, with salt and pepper hair cut neatly, tanned skin, and a tattoo of a guitar on his forearm. A tattoo? None of the professional portraits hanging in Granny's living room show his tattoos.

I watch, awed, as he sets a bowl of salad on the table and then cracks open two beers, giving one to Granny. Holy crap, my grandfather is cool.

"Hi, there," he says, noticing me for the first time. His smile is wide, his teeth white. "I'm Joe."

"Emma," I say, steadying my muscles as I reach out to shake his hand. There's another tattoo on his other arm, several circles in a vertical line, a line of dots connecting them. I'd recognize it anywhere. The planets, nine of them, and then the sun. My astronomy-loving heart squeezes at the sight of Pluto, the dwarf planet that has been stricken off the planets list in my time. I reach up and touch my taurus necklace, grateful that it time traveled with me. "Nice tattoo."

"Thanks. You got any ink?"

"Not yet," I say. Uncle Ray kicks my shin under the table. A quiet, annoying way of telling me to shut up.

I grab a kebob and take a bite, sitting back in my

chair and becoming a silent observer of my family's dinnertime conversation. Granny talks about her work at the library, complaining about the constant lack of funding.

My grandfather reaches for another kebab. "Ray, how was work today?"

"It was fine. Slow. I don't know how we stay in business."

"I blame that pizza chain for showing up across town and dragging all your customers away," Joe says. "Why do people like that cardboard shit anyhow? Magic Mark's is real, homemade pizza."

"It's so much better," Granny agrees.

"Just stick to what you do," Joe says, taking another sip of his beer. "Make a quality product and never sacrifice your integrity. People will take notice."

"As long as I keep getting a paycheck, I'm happy," Ray says with a snort. "Cornell isn't cheap. Oh, and Emma actually gave away a free pizza today."

I roll my eyes. "I had no choice! You left me alone and that Marci girl looked like she was about to go all Karen on me."

"Who's Karen?" Granny asks.

"No one. It's an expression. It just means … like an annoying customer."

Ray snorts. "Marci is fine as long as she's not with her idiot boyfriend."

"Marci? Isn't she Betsy Hill's kid?" Granny's look sours as she cuts into her asparagus, sawing the butter knife harder than necessary. "I don't trust those people. They're—"

"Honey," Joe says, a loving tone spoken as a word of caution. "Maybe we should talk about something more interesting with our guest here."

"Oh, it's no problem," I say over a mouthful of

shrimp. "I love gossip."

My future grandparents chuckle. Ray shoots me a warning glance. He's been on edge all night, and while I get where he's coming from about the whole time continuum thing, it's hard to pull myself away from Granny and Joe. I want to sit here, eating dinner and having mundane chats for as long as I possibly can, but it only turns out to be an hour, if that.

Then dinner is over, and I have no excuse to hang around the two family members who don't know they're my family. Once night falls and they go to bed, Ray and I sneak into the kitchen and boot up the computer.

"Okay," he whispers, fingers on the keyboard while I sit next to him on a kitchen chair. "Let's set my away status…"

I watch quietly while he tinkers around on this vintage internet software called AOL. Finally, Google loads. He types: *accidental time travel into the past*

I'm pretty sure there's no way to Google ourselves out of this predicament, and if there is, the answer is likely to be in my 2024 version of Google, not his. The internet has come a long way in twenty years, but even if time travel was a readily accessible thing, I'm pretty sure I would have heard about it by now. I can already picture all the TikTok trends that would explode once time travel became a thing. Travelers from the future would be instant celebrities. Pranks would be taken to the next level.

"We can't freak out about this," I whisper in the darkness. The only light is the glow of the computer monitor which Ray has dimmed down as low as it goes.

"No one is freaking out," he whispers back. He looks over. "Are you freaking out?"

I shake my head. It's only a half-lie. "Last night I fell asleep in my mom's old bed and woke up in the same place but twenty years in the past. If I just go back to sleep tonight, maybe I'll wake up in the future. Maybe it'll all go back to normal."

"You're assuming you time traveled as a fluke, then?"

"What do you mean?"

Ray's brows pull together as he thinks. "You didn't purposely time travel, so that leaves only two other explanations … a fluke, or a reason."

"What could the reason possibly be?" I ask, my voice barely above a whisper.

"Maybe it's something only the universe knows."

"Maybe," I say, ignoring the chills that prickle across my shoulders. "More likely it's just a fluke."

I am just one boring girl. What could the universe possibly want with me?

"I hope so," Ray says. "I was thinking you could just sleep in the top bunk in my room but maybe you should stay in Lindsey's bed just in case. She's not here, so she'll never know."

"That's a good idea."

We exhaust Google's results for two hours, but don't find anything of value. We finally call it quits well past midnight. Uncle Ray leans against Mom's bedroom door, lingering while I pull back the sheets on her bed.

"I hope this works," I say, trying to instill at least a small bit of confidence in my voice. "With any luck, you won't see me tomorrow."

He grins. "And then, what, I guess I just wait the next twenty years?"

"Well, you'll see me when I'm born."

"Yeah, but in your timeline, this doesn't happen until you're seventeen. So in my timeline, I'll have to wait until you turn seventeen and then…?" He blows out a deep breath of air and shakes his head. "Time travel is terrifying."

"Tell me about it," I say. "Well … goodnight."

"Goodnight," he says, turning toward the hall. He stops, turning back to me, his teeth digging into his bottom lip. "Hey, Emma?"

"Yes?"

He watches me for a moment, then looks at the floor. "Am I happy in the future?"

"What do you mean?"

His mouth opens, and then closes. He shakes his head. "Never mind. Don't answer. I'm not supposed to know. Goodnight, Emma."

Chapter Six

Phone addiction is a real thing, and my dependence is bone deep. After lying in this unfamiliar, messy bedroom for an hour, unsuccessfully trying to fall asleep, I realize I need my phone. I've never gone so long without looking at it before. And seriously, Mom's room is a mess. She has no business telling me to keep mine clean now that I know how she lived back in the day.

Carefully, I tiptoe to the next bedroom and take my phone from its hiding spot in Ray's shelf while he softly snores from his bottom bunk. Without any service, there's obviously no new messages, no missed calls, no notifications of any kind. Back in Mom's bed, I take a deep breath, clutching this one piece of my old life in my hands. Inside are pictures of the life I left behind, the life I know existed before I woke up in the past. All the problems I thought I had just two days ago are nothing compared to being stuck in the year 2004.

This is bananas.

I would love to go back to my time and be the heartbroken jobless loser again. That would be fantastic.

You hear that, Universe? Please send me back!

Jumping out of the bed, I push Mom's door closed and twist the lock. Then I crawl back into the soft jersey sheets and unlock my phone, desperate to interact with a device from my own time.

I tap the text message icon, even though I know it'll only remind me of Jonah's treacherous deeds that caused my heart to break. I tell myself I'll just read over Nina's texts because I miss her, and all her texts are kind and loving to me. Reading her texts will make me happy, unlike when I read my loser ex-boyfriend's old texts. But, true to Emma Fitzgerald fashion, as soon as the app opens, my eyes fix on Jonah's name. I blink.

He's Jonah heart emoji again. Not a single poop emoji in sight.

How did that happen?

I tap the text thread.

Jonah: **k, call me when you're done. love you!**

I scroll up.

Jonah: **I'm thinking Mexican food tonight. Taco truck or sit down place?**

Emma: **taco truckkkkkkkk**

Jonah: **lol bet**

Jonah: **pick you up at 6?**

Emma: **yup**

My throat goes dry. I look up, almost expecting to see the entire room transformed, but it's still Mom's teenager room, the same as it was a minute ago. I'm still in 2004. I scroll back down, then up, and the texts don't change. Jonah's name has the heart emoji next to it. I swipe out of the text app and refresh my phone. Same thing. Where the hell did the poop emoji go? Where are his horrible breakup texts? The words I've memorized down to every last punctuation mark?

I click on Nina's texts and they all seem normal. I can't remember the last thing we texted each other in my timeline because it didn't matter because she didn't break my heart... I haven't obsessed over her texts for the last week, so if something's changed, I can't tell. I scroll up, through yesterday and the day before, passing memes and random texts from my best friend. Nothing unusual pops out at me, until I realize the string of memes Nina had made a few days ago aren't there. They were hilarious. They were all about Addy, in Nina's snarky attempt to cheer me up after our former friend ruined my life. They're gone now.

I search through the rest of my phone. Addy's

texts are also gone. We hadn't communicated much in the last month, but we used to have a chain of texts before she started working on her dad's campaign. I know I didn't delete them because I kept thinking I could perform a text autopsy, determining the exact moment that my friend had decided to steal my boyfriend.

I can't find a single photo of her, either. Her bright blonde hair and ocean blue eyes are nowhere on my phone's camera roll. She's not on my Snapchat friends list.

Addy is nowhere.

I turn off my phone and turn it back on again, but it doesn't make Jonah's texts go back to normal. It doesn't make Addy come back. My phone seems to have erased all evidence of Addyson Deblois.

It's like she never existed.

****

"Well, damn."

I blink awake to Uncle Ray's face.

Uncle Ray's *teenage* face. He's wearing a Star Trek t-shirt and red and blue plaid pajama pants, a look of utter disappointment on his face.

I sit up in Mom's bed for the second morning in a row, yawning because it took me forever to fall asleep last night. It's kind of hard to blissfully pass out when you're hoping sleep will transport you twenty years into the future. I can say with one thousand percent certainty, it's harder to fall asleep under these conditions than any childhood Christmas Eve or night before my birthday.

"Help me, Obi-wan Kenobi," I say, giving him a sad smile. "You're my only hope."

"Hell yeah! Star Wars is still cool in the future."

I grin. Uncle Ray's favorite character, Din Djarin, is still years away from his TV debut here in 2004. I wish I could tell Ray about the Mandalorian, but I hold back, knowing we'll have tons of nerding out to do in the future.

"Guess you're coming with me to work again," he says, tapping the door frame. "Mom and Dad are at work already, so we'll avoid them as much as possible."

I frown. "I like hanging out with them, though."

He holds up a finger. "Nuh-uh. No sad face. We can't manipulate the future, so you have to keep away from everyone but me."

My half-awake consciousness snaps fully awake. The future. I grab my phone, which is next to my pillow—Mom's pillow—and turn it on.

"Dude, I told you to hide that thing," Ray panic-whispers.

"Sorry. I'll only be a second."

I check the texts and it's the same from last night. Addyson is gone. A cold, thrilling flutter flaps through my veins.

"It's been a second," Ray says, narrowing his eyes at me before turning away. "Hide that thing before I'm done with my hair. And wear your Magic Mark's shirt again today."

"That thing smells like pizza," I whine.

"Good thing you'll be at a pizza restaurant!" he calls back.

For the second morning in a row, I watch my uncle flat iron his hair and then emerge from his room wearing the same shirt as me plus a pair of navy blue Dickie's work pants and his Converse. I'd be a little terrified that not only have I time traveled, but I might be stuck in a Groundhog Day situation, but Ray is a part of it, too. I shudder at the thought of reliving every day over and over again. No thanks. Time travel is better, although still horrifying.

I hope I find a way to go back home before the

summer is over, otherwise Ray will have a hard time hiding me in his dorm room at Cornell. I push the thoughts from my mind. I can't stay here, hidden away from society, forever. I just can't.

Ray checks out his hair in the car mirror every single time he comes to a stop on the short drive to work. He brushes his sharply-flat bangs over to the left, then the right, then practices with them kind of directly in his eyes.

"Your curls are so nice," I say. "Why do you flatten your hair each day?"

"It's cool. It's punk rock." His eyes meet mine in the Mustang's rear-view mirror and he shrugs. "Everyone does it—even the straight guys."

"Have you thought about coming out?" I ask.

The look he flashes me tells me I should probably just shut up. So I do.

It's Tuesday, another weekday, where Ray works the day shift all by himself, so once again he hides me out in the back office. I sit in the dirty office chair and spin around aimlessly, look at the paper timecards hanging on the wall, and flip through a Magic Mark's franchise catalog. One of those old school calculators that print on a roll of paper beckons to me from the boss' desk, but as much fun as it looks, I don't play with it. For all I know, using up a few inches of calculator paper might forever ruin the future.

Right. The future.

I've been trying to put it out of my mind, but I can't. Addyson is gone, and although I don't know why, it has to be my fault. I did something to mess up the time continuum and I don't even know what it was. The real question, I guess, is what happened to Addy? How could I have done something to make us never be friends in the future? What did I do that stopped her from applying for the internship at the observatory and then stealing Jonah away from me?

It doesn't make sense. Addy is my age, so she hasn't even been born yet in this time. A customer enters the restaurant and Uncle Ray tells them their pizza is almost ready. As the door closes, the bells smack against the glass, triggering memories of yesterday.

I talked to someone yesterday. I gave her free pizza.

I wait motionless in the back office until I hear the bells ring again. With the customer gone, I peek out into the front area where Ray is doodling on an order pad.

"Hey," I say, glancing around the restaurant. "This place is empty, right?"

"Yeah," he says, nodding for me to join him. "You want pizza? I'm about to make one for lunch."

"I have a question." I choose my words carefully. If Ray knows I might have messed up the timeline, he might spontaneously combust, which would be a huge health hazard. Not to mention, a gigantic blunder in the time continuum.

"That girl I gave the free pizza to yesterday?"

"Marci," he says, his gaze looking out the wall of windows at the front of the restaurant. "What about her? I've been stressing about it, too, but hopefully a free pizza didn't mess up too much."

"What was it Granny had said about her?"

He cocks an eyebrow, confused. "Dot," I say. "Your mom."

"Right ... Granny." He shakes his head like he doesn't quite believe it. "Marci's parents are big wigs in the town. Bunch a jerks, if you ask me. Why?"

I shrug, l hoping I look bored instead of curious out of my mind. "What do you know about her? She didn't really seem like she belonged in Pine Grove. She was so fancy and preppy. I feel like she'd rather be in Hollywood."

He snorts. "She was the most popular girl in school since, well, forever. She's dating this dude named Donovan. But they're both rich so it's not like the ten bucks she saved from a free pizza will change her life. I think we're in the clear."

"Cool," I say, trying to figure out what this girl has to do with Addyson's missing texts. Marci and Donovan sound so familiar, like the words to an old song I haven't heard in years. *Marci and Donovan.*

Uncle Ray goes back to doodling on the order pad—tiny little squares in the margins, every other one colored in like a checkerboard. The girl I gave a pizza to yesterday would be my parents' age in my time, yet Marci and Donovan, two names that mean nothing separately seem so familiar when put together. I know I've heard it before. Or seen it.

Then it hits me. The memory my brain just recalled comes to me in Nina's mocking voice.

"Next year's Cypress High prom will be held at the Moody Convention Center, courtesy of a generous donation from Marci and Donovan Deblois."

"Ugh," Nina had said, just a few weeks ago while we walked to first period. "What's wrong with the gym that we use every year for prom? They could be donating that money to feed starving children, but *no*, they have to uproot our entire prom just to show off how much money they can afford to throw away." She crumpled up the prom flyer and tossed it into a nearby trashcan. "I don't know how you're friends with Addyson. She's the worst."

"It's not her fault her parents are rich," I'd said, naively sticking up for my semi-friend in the weeks before she'd ruined my life. Addy was my school friend, but Nina was my best friend. My Bestie. BFFs. There's a big difference.

A prickly sensation covers my whole body. I start to feel a little seasick, despite my feet being firmly on the tile floor. The girl I gave a free pizza to yesterday is Addyson's future mom.

The girl I encouraged to break up with her boyfriend.

Addyson isn't just missing from my phone in the future. It's not that we never became friends. Addyson Deblois has never been born because I broke up her parents.

Does that make me a murderer? My chest constricts, but I push the thoughts away. No, of course I'm not a murderer. You can't kill someone who doesn't even exist yet.

"Whoa."

"What?" Ray says.

Shit. I hadn't realized I'd spoken out loud. "Nothing," I say quickly, bracing for his questions. I am a terrible liar. He's going to find out what I did, and he'll be livid.

Several moments pass. Uncle Ray says nothing. I glance over at him and he's staring out the front windows, doodling-pen resting in his hand. I follow his gaze and watch a muscular Black guy with dark skin walk across the parking lot. His dark hair is cut very short. He slips a baseball cap on his head as he approaches the shopping center, walking toward the music store. The cap has the music store logo on it, and I realize it's matching his polo shirt, which is barely squeezed over his incredible muscles.

My uncle watches this guy the way I used to watch Jonah. The way I still watch Andre from Zombie Radio when Nina and I see them perform live.

I decide I'm not going to tell him about Addyson. What's done is done, after all. And besides, maybe the great controller of the Universe set this all up on purpose. Maybe Ray was supposed to leave me all alone yesterday and I was supposed to meet Marci. The Universe would know that I'd be compelled to tell someone to break up with a partner who didn't treat them right. Maybe this is all going according to some weird cosmic plan, so no, Ray doesn't need to know.

I'm the one who time traveled. I deserve to have a better life when I get back.

Right?

Chapter Seven

Pine Grove starts to look just like how I remember it once we've driven out of the main part of the town. Miles of cow pastures float past my window as we cruise down Highway 336, the vast flat land dotted with a random pine tree or cow every so often. The other side of the road has sparsely populated homes, set far back from the road, usually surrounded with an ornate metal fence. Nestled at the edge of town, just before the trees thicken and the national forest begins, is Pine Grove Estates, the subdivision where my grandparents raised their family.

I don't know why they tacked the word "estates" onto the brick sign at the front of the neighborhood. The homes here are solidly working-class ranch-style homes that were built in the eighties.

"The longer you're here, the more you risk changing the future," Ray says as he cruises with one hand slung over the steering wheel, the other on the stick shift. "We have to find a way to get you back."

"Agreed." I turn away from my window and smile. "Although it's been really fun spending two days with you at work. Boring, but also fun to see how things work in this time."

He snorts. "It's good luck that Ty is on vacation this week, otherwise it'd be tricky keeping you away from him. Dude can talk. Hopefully we'll get you back to your time before he returns to work."

"I've been thinking," I say, taking a breath to slow the increase in my heartbeat. "Remember how you said this could be a fluke or a reason? What if I was sent back here for a reason? Like, what if the universe wants me to change the timeline, and you're doing all this worrying for nothing?"

"Nope. Hell, no." He shakes his head. "The Universe doesn't work like that."

"How do you know? Maybe that's exactly how it works."

He doesn't even pretend to consider my theory. His head only shakes even more. "There's no way. If everyone just traveled back in time all willy-nilly to change something, then the Universe would combust. The time continuum is a very precious thing. For all we know, just you and I hanging out right now could have devastating consequences."

His cheeks puff up as he blows out a breath. "I've been stressing about it a lot, which is saying something because I'm usually too stressed about other things to stress even more about new things."

"What are you stressed about?" I ask. "Are you nervous about starting Cornell in the fall?"

"Not really, but now I am." He gives me a scornful look, then turns back ahead, tapping his blinker to turn into Pine Grove Estates.

"So what are you stressed about?" I press.

"I don't want to talk about it. All I know is we have to get you back to 2024. No offense or anything—I like hanging out with you, but yeah."

I've been thinking about it, too, but not the way my uncle has. I'm thrilled. I'm giddy and excited to go back to my time. A new, better time where Addyson doesn't exist. Where Jonah and I are still a happy couple. *This* is what the Universe wanted me to do. There's no other reason for me to have traveled back twenty years. Plus, there have been too many coincidences that fell into place perfectly—my mom is out of town this week so I can sleep in her bed, Ray's coworker is on vacation so he can bring me to work, and let's not forget the one very big thing—the Universe sent Marci to me directly, knowing I'd tell her to break up with Donovan. And it did that *while* Ray wasn't in the restaurant.

The Universe clearly planned this. And it's all going perfectly.

Now I just have to find my way back home.

"It's Tuesday, so my parents are at bingo tonight," Ray says as he turns into the empty driveway. "We need to—"

"They're at *what*?" I say, bursting into laughter. Granny is way too classy to play Bingo.

"Bingo?" Ray parks his car. "It's this game with a board of numbers … you don't have Bingo in the future? It's really popular."

"I know what Bingo is. I just can't picture Granny playing it."

He rolls his eyes. Inside, Ray closes the front door, locks it, and clasps his hands together in front of his chest. He's still wearing his Magic Mark's baseball cap on top of his flat hair. Yesterday he hung it from the rear-view mirror of the Mustang.

"Okay. Let's be smart about this. You time traveled here and don't know how." His eyes alight with mischief. "We need to find the portal."

"What's a portal look like?"

"I don't know. It's probably invisible. And it's most likely in Lindsey's bedroom since that's where you appeared."

"What if the entire house is a portal?" It's a scary thought that I could suddenly blink out of existence and appear in another time.

Ray looks up at the ceiling, then back at me. "Let's start small."

We check Mom's room first.

I pull a pair of black foam shoes out from under the bed. They're three inches tall with a foam strap across the top that's made of some kind of holographic plastic. It's delightfully tacky. Old school raver chic.

"Nina would love these."

"Who's Nina?" Ray asks me from the other side of the bed. He's also on the floor, pressing his hands to each plank of hardwood flooring.

I smile, tossing the shoes aside. "My bestie. We've been besties since Ms. Morgan's kindergarten class."

"Don't throw those," he says. Put them back exactly where you found them. What if Lindsey trips over it or something? That'll change the timeline."

I resist rolling my eyes and put the shoes back where I found them, approximately three inches from the edge of the bed, bent at a forty-five-degree angle from the footboard.

"Is Nina a raver?" Ray asks a few seconds later.

"Nope." I chuckle at the idea of my beautiful Latina best friend rocking the neon puffy pants and glow stick aesthetic. She'd hate it. "She's athletic. Laid back. Super casual with her fashion sense, but she's a huge dork for tacky stuff like that. The girl loves her slides."

"Hmm," he says, crawling down toward the foot of the bed, tapping each floor plank.

Maybe we're doing something wrong, but the floor under Mom's bed does not contain a portal. We check the wall behind her headboard next, pulling out the bed frame a bit to see it all, both of us pressing our hands to the drywall. Uncle Ray feels all along the wooden headboard, footboard, and even underneath her mattress. We find a hundred dollar bill stashed under there but not a portal.

"I feel bad," I say, after lowering the mattress. "I don't like snooping through her stuff."

He just shrugs. "Lindsey and I are really close. If

she knew the reason why we needed to go through her stuff, she'd be fine with it."

We press on just about every square inch of floor, wall, and ceiling in Mom's room and don't find anything. Then we move to Ray's room which shares a wall with Mom's. He drags his dresser across the floor, and we stare at the dark blue wall for a long moment.

He shrugs hair from his eyes and brings his thumbnail up to his teeth. "If this doesn't work, I don't know what will."

"Don't lose hope." I press my palms to the wall, wishing they'd slip right through and transport me back to my own time so I can start my life back over the right way, with Jonah by my side. When nothing happens, I swallow my disappointment and look at my uncle. "Princes Leia never lost hope."

He grins. "I'm glad my sister raised you on Star Wars."

"You did, actually."

I'm expecting another round of *don't tell me*, but he just goes to work looking for the portal we still haven't been able to find. An hour later, our search has yielded exactly two missing socks, a NYC pin-back button, a forgotten CD mixtape, and zero time travel devices or magical wormhole portals.

"Let's check the breaker box," Ray says, eyebrows disappearing into his swoopy bangs. "Maybe time travel has something to do with electricity."

Chills prickle across my neck. "Wait ... I have an idea."

"Let's hear it, dawg."

"There's a barn in the back yard, right?"

"Yes."

"The telescope," I say. "It created pink smoke the day I time traveled. But as soon as I walked up to it, it disappeared. It was really, really weird."

"We don't have a telescope," he says, frowning.

"Is there a bunch of junk in the barn?"

He nods.

"Let's go check."

Of all the things that are different from this world to my own, the barn looks largely the same. Only it's missing that telescope. We look all over, peering in boxes and crawling through the forgotten flea market treasures my grandparents have collected over the years. There is no freaking telescope to be found.

Granny had said the telescope belonged to my grandfather. And while I don't say it out loud, I know my grandfather dies in three years from a heart attack no one saw coming. That's three years I might be stuck here in the past, waiting for him to find it and bring it home to the barn of curiosities.

After every single item has been touched, lifted, and pushed aside, I curse under my breath. "It's not here."

The sound of a car approaching makes my uncle curse under his breath. "My parents must be home early. We need to get out of here and sneak you back in my room so you don't unwittingly change the future."

It's an easy enough task to rush back into the house through the back door, but as soon as I'm secure in Ray's bedroom, busying myself by looking through his CD collection, I hear a voice that is definitely not Granny's.

It's my mom.

"Dude!" she yells out from across the house. "Bro-seph! Hurry and get out here. Mom waxed the floor!"

Ray's eyes widen and he looks over at me, putting a finger to his lips. "Don't leave my room. She can't see you."

The bedroom door flings open.

Too late.

My mom stands there, twenty-one years old. Pale skin, freckled cheeks, long auburn hair tied in a low ponytail. She wears a Zombie Radio t-shirt that's been cut down the sides and tied in knots to cling tightly to her body, and black skinny jeans with scrappy holes in the knees. Her feet are bare, her toes bright red. Her eyes, the same bright green I remember, are rimmed with smokey eyeshadow.

"Whoops," she says, putting a hand over her eyes. "Didn't realize you had a girl here."

Ray rushes up to the door, but my mom pushes past him, holding out her hand to me. "Hi, I'm Lindsey."

"Emma," I say, having no choice but to shake her hand. Meeting my own mom before she's even met the man who will become my father is totally not a risk to the time continuum, right?

"Ooh, pretty name!"

Behind her, Ray looks absolutely panicked. I think I even see a sheen of sweat on his forehead.

"Dudes!" she says, eyes wide with mischief. "Mom waxed the floor!"

Only she means *her* mom. Time travel is weird.

"Nice," Ray says, still hovering by the door like he's trying to get her to leave. "We're kind of busy but maybe later—"

"No way," Mom says. "Newly waxed kitchen floor means one thing and one thing only, dammit."

My uncle rolls his eyes. "Lindsey…"

"I won't live here forever, little bro-seph. I'm moving out soon and you're going to college, and then you'll miss our days of epic sock surfing. You'll say, gosh I wish I'd sock surfed every chance I got."

"Sock surfing?" My jaw drops. Sock surfing is only the happiest memory my mom and uncle talk about all the time. I've heard this story more often than I've heard about my mom's epic summer spent traveling around Texas following Zombie Radio's tour. Once a year my grandmother would clean and wax the linoleum kitchen floor, making it extra slippery. Mom and Ray would wear socks and slide around, making a game out of it.

Apparently once my grandparents got new tile flooring, the days of sock surfing were over and forever missed. They still reminisce about it sometimes.

Ray glares daggers at me, but I can't help myself. I stand up. "I want to sock surf!"

"*Yes,*" Mom says, yanking open Ray's top dresser drawer. She grabs two pairs of socks and tosses one to me. "Let's go."

"This is so not a good idea," Ray hisses in my ear as I follow my future mother down the hallway and to the kitchen. I'm still in awe as I look around at the house that is so familiar and yet so foreign at the same time.

We sock up and Mom—or Lindsey, though it's hard to think of her as anything other than Mom—stands at the line where the living room carpet stops and the kitchen linoleum begins. She lifts her arms, Lion King style. The only thing she's missing is a baby Simba.

"Fine people of the house, I happily present to you, the 2004 Sock Surfing Olympics. You won't find skill of this measure at the games in Greece. You won't find abs like Michael Phelps here, either."

With a flourish of her hands, she runs and slides across the floor, her socks carrying her at least fifteen feet before she smoothly smacks into the wall on the other side of the kitchen. No lie, I am *impressed.*

"Sock surfing!" she says in a low, guttural rally

cry.

"All right, all right, I'm in," Ray says, pulling his skinny jeans up a few inches and bending at the knees, like an athlete getting ready to compete. He backs up, then takes a running start across the living room carpet, throwing up his arms. "Sock surfing!"

Lindsey points at me, her back still pressed against the wall. "Your turn, new girl."

I look at Ray. He's doing a moonwalk on the slippery floor, holding onto Lindsey's shoulder for support. I can't believe he's okay with this. What if I fall and crack my head open? The hospital would have no identification for me and the time continuum would change far worse than the tiny change I've already made to it.

"Sock surfing," Lindsey chants, pumping her fists in the air. "Sock surfing! Come on, new girl, show us what you got."

"I dunno," I say, standing at the edge of the carpet, Ray's thick socks covering all the way to my calves. "I don't want to get hurt."

"Sock surfing is a lover, not a fighter," Ray says. He turns around and moonwalks toward me. I had no idea he could do this, by the way.

Meeting me at the carpet, he holds out his hand, and I reach for it. "Lindsey? Can I get some tunes?"

She skates across the kitchen, where a thin white stereo is mounted up under the kitchen cabinets. With the press of a button, an electronic pop song blasts through the room. Ray grabs my other hand and pulls me onto the linoleum. His smirk is carefree, happy. It's the first time his face hasn't been pinched in confusion or stress since I showed up in my teenage mom's bedroom one random morning.

"Hold on to me," he says, shimmying his feet

across the slippery floor. "I won't let you fall."

Before I became a time traveler, I would have embraced sock surfing with no fear because falling to the floor probably won't cause much damage. But now I'm worried because I've seen how the simple act of telling a girl to ditch her boyfriend can prevent my worst enemy from being born.

That happens to be a really good consequence of changing the timeline. It's probably the reason the Universe sent me here in the first place. But I can't tempt fate twice. I would be taking the gift the Universe gave me and throwing it away. I let my uncle swing me across the room, never loosening my grip on him. After a few moments of silly dancing to the music, I realize there's not much to fear. The floor is silky smooth, but it's not like it's truly as slippery as an ice-skating rink.

"Okay," I say, releasing Ray's hands after the second song we've slow-shimmied to. "I think I've got my bearings. And now I'm about to rock your socks off with my incredible talent."

He cups his hands to his mouth and deepens his voice, calling out to an invisible crowd of imaginary spectators. "Listen up, dedicated fans of Sock Surfing 2004, we have a brand new contestant. Please welcome Emma!"

Lindsey's finger hovers over the radio. "What kind of music would you like for your performance?"

"Umm ... classical?"

She quirks an eyebrow but presses a button and the soothing sound of a slow classical song floods into the room. I stand at the edge where the carpet meets the linoleum and close my eyes. Part of it is for dramatics, and part of it is to have a small moment with myself. *Is this really happening? Am I about to do a silly dance across the kitchen twenty years into the past?*

I open my eyes.

Yep. That's exactly what I'm going to do.

I only took figure skating lessons for two years in fifth and sixth grade before deciding that I'd much rather be a famous dirt bike racer, so I quit and begged my parents for a dirt bike. It didn't work. But I'm sure I still have some skills from sixth grade buried in my muscle memory.

With a leap, I skip onto the kitchen floor, do a couple swizzle slides, then whip my body into an advanced two-foot spin. My cheering audience of two people applaud and whoop, which only encourages me to show off a little more. At the edge of the room, I skate forward, hold out my arms and twist my body into a spin, lifting my right foot to rest on my knee. I make it four or five turns before the friction slows me down.

When I open my eyes, the room spins. I crash lightly into the wall, then throw my hands up in victory.

"Damn, new girl," Lindsey says, switching the music back to an alternative rock station. "Ray, she's so out of your league."

"We're not dating," I say.

"Just friends," my uncle confirms.

Lindsey cocks her head, looking from her brother to me, like she's not the least bit convinced. "I dunno. Seems like you two are hiding something."

"Nah," Ray says. A little too quickly. A little too suspiciously. "Just friends."

She narrows her eyes. My heart races. In my time, my mom is a woman who refuses to let things go. She's got a rock-solid intuition and she trusts it completely. If teenage Lindsey is anything like my adult mom, we are in huge danger of being found out.

"We are hiding something," I blurt out.

Ray gives me a death glare, which doesn't look

73

too intimidating on him. I've never been able to lie successfully to my mom, but I have to do something.

"My boyfriend broke up with me," I say, chewing on the inside of my lip to look convincing. After all, every good lie is rooted in truth. "I'm still heartbroken over it and I just don't want my family to worry about me, so … Ray said I could hang out with him for a while."

Lindsay watches me, weighing my words against her natural lie detector. After a few seconds she shrugs. "Fine. Don't tell me the real truth."

Chapter Eight

I am awake. I've been awake. I'm not entirely sure I'm even capable of falling asleep. My uncle, who is too afraid of the time-continuum, had told his parents that I was feeling sick and would be taking my dinner in his room, so I didn't get to hang out with my grandparents. I'm still stewing over it when he comes to bed, dropping down on the bottom bunk like he's just suffered through the longest, most exhausting day of his life. He falls asleep instantly, leaving me here, awake. Thinking about Jonah.

We're back together now, in the future, where I belong. He loves me and I love him, and Addy doesn't exist, which means I'll probably still get my summer internship when I go back. I'm so giddy I can't stand it. I am full on toddler-levels of giddy and it's nearly impossible to sleep.

I left 2024 as a heartbroken mess, but now I get to return happy again. Whole. Back together, but better. The Universe gave me this amazing gift.

I just have to figure out how to go back.

As soon as the barest inkling of the sun's morning rays peeks through the curtains, I sling half my body off the top bunk and stare at my uncle. He's passed out, face squished into the pillow, back rising and falling with each breath of deep sleep. I clear my throat. He doesn't move.

The digital alarm clock on his nightstand tells me it's 6:00 in the morning. He works every Monday through Friday during the summer, eight hours a day, which leaves very little time for us to find the portal so I can get back home. I need to get back home, now more than ever. My mission is complete, Jonah is mine again, and all my memories of Addyson are just horrible dreams from the past that no longer exist. I am ready to step back into a more perfect version of my life in the year 2024.

"Ahem!"

Ray's deep, quiet snoring doesn't falter. I tap on the metal bunk bed frame with my fingernails. His breath hitches, but not enough for him to wake up.

I roll back onto my bed and groan. I'll never find the time travel portal just lying in bed and hanging out with Ray at his pizza job five days a week. I slide off the top bunk, feet dropping to the floor with a soft thud that still doesn't wake him.

While I hadn't done anything specifically to make myself time travel on purpose, I still ended up here after falling asleep in my time. My fingers slide across my Taurus necklace. I'm starting to think the stars have something to do with this. It's not just a time continuum—it's a *space* time continuum. Even the great Stephen Hawking talked about the possibility of time travel by bending space and time in such a way that it looped back over each other. Maybe some cosmic twist of space-time caused me to accidentally time travel.

Or, no. It wouldn't be an accident. I think the Universe did this on purpose to give me a second chance at happiness. It might seem selfish to think the universe would choose me and my teenage heartbreak as the problem to fix, but it also makes sense. In the days after my breakup with Jonah, I'd spent every night on the roof of the Infinity Motel, staring up at the stars and wishing I had Jonah back. Intense neediness is a typical Taurus trait, and I longed for a life where I didn't have to miss him so much.

For all I know, a week of sending my longing feelings out into the Universe made the Universe answer back.

I pull out my phone. It's worthless for finding

new information since the 5G network doesn't connect to anything and there's no Wi-Fi in this house, but my moon phases app still works. I scroll all the way to 2024, to the exact date I left my world and woke up in this one.

It was Sunday, June 2nd. A Waning Crescent moon. The moon was in Aries. I rock back on my heels.

It means nothing.

You'd think something as spectacular as time travel would happen during a New Moon, or a Full Moon. Maybe an eclipse. Especially during an eclipse. But the day I left my own time wasn't of any noteworthy importance to the universe. I scroll back to the date I arrived, and it was a Waning Gibbous moon.

Also nothing special.

Rolling back and forth on my heels, I exhale a mountain of frustration. The perfect future I want is waiting for me … twenty years away.

I read over Jonah's new texts until I have them memorized, wishing they'd erase the memories of the texts he'd sent me before I time traveled. My heart squeezes at the pixels on the screen. Simple ones and zeros that display his love for me. In my camera roll, I look back at the photos we've taken over the past couple of years together, smiling at one from a few months ago when I went with him to a cooking class that was offered at some prestigious culinary school downtown.

I zoom in on his face. Silky black hair that always smelled like vanilla because he shared a shampoo bottle with his little sister, Tala. That little smirk of a grin he wore so well. His rich brown eyes seem to stare right into my soul even from beyond a pixelated screen. Jonah and I cooked bihon pancit that night, a traditional Filipino dish.

I'd told him he was cheating because he made pancit meals with his mom at home all the time. But he was really excited to learn how to make the noodles from scratch with flour, eggs, and salt instead of using the premade dry noodles at home.

I smile at the memories as I flip through the few pictures I took of that night. Halfway through the class, my hands were too dirty to touch my phone, but it didn't matter because I'd already snapped the cutest photo of Jonah sticking his tongue out at me while wearing his tall papery chef's hat.

We had been so perfect together. I don't know why he would ever choose Addyson over me. Is she prettier? More fun to be around? It's almost like I can hear Nina's voice in my ear anytime I start to think things like this.

"Hell no, sis. You're a ten. Always."

I draw in a deep breath and shake my head. It doesn't matter. Addy is no longer my problem. I touch Jonah's face on my phone screen, wishing I were touching the real thing. Feeling his soft stubble on my fingertips. Leaning in close, pressing my lips to his. I miss every single thing about him.

"I'm coming for you, Jonah."

Uncle Ray sits up in bed, the sudden sound startling me. "Why are you talking about your ex?"

"Huh?" I turn off my phone screen and stash it back behind sci-fi books. "Nothing."

"You said 'I'm coming for you Jonah'." He narrows his eyes. "Please tell me you're not planning on killing him when you get back."

I snort out a laugh. "Definitely not! I love him."

Exactly half a second too late, I realize my mistake. And one second after that, I know my stupid expressive face just gave away everything.

"Why would you say that?" Ray says, smacking his clock when the alarm starts buzzing. "Why would you

THE YEARS BETWEEN US

even consider taking someone back after they left you for someone else?"

His lip curls in disgust. "You need to walk away from that, Emma. Burn the bridge. Never go back."

"It's not like that."

"Then please enlighten me." He walks over to his closet and starts getting ready for work. "You're my niece and I know that your mom and I would have raised you better than that. We are bridge burners, Emma. If someone hurts you like that, you burn the bridge and walk away, you don't ever take them back."

"Maybe he hasn't actually hurt me," I say, sitting on Ray's desk chair. "Maybe the future doesn't have to stay the same."

Ray pulls a Magic Mark's Pizza shirt over his head. "What the hell does that mean?"

"I have to tell you something."

His eyes widen. "Oh, god. What?"

"It's totally not a big deal." I'm talking too fast, but I can't help it. If I can convince him that this is a good thing, maybe he'll chill out about not wanting to mess up the time continuum. I put on a smile as my uncle just glares at me. "And I think it's what the universe wanted, anyway. So it's a good thing."

"What is it?"

"Don't get mad."

He drops his forehead into his palm. "What did you do? Just tell me. Maybe it won't be that bad."

"My mortal enemy has disappeared from my phone. All evidence that she even exists is gone, which means she's never born in my time."

"No way." His palms press to his temples. Then he looks at me incredulously. "How did sock surfing with Lindsey do that?"

I swallow. "It didn't."

"Dude." He throws his arms up in the air. I think I even see a vein bulging in his forehead. He's taking this way too seriously.

"I might have broken up Marci and her boyfriend that day I gave her the free pizza."

"What!" he whisper-yells, glancing nervously at his closed door.

"She was complaining about her boyfriend and I told her she shouldn't date someone like that, and then later on I realized she marries him in my timeline and they give birth to a heinous demon named Addyson who grows up and pretends to be my friend then stabs me in the back."

"You. Can't. Change. The. Timeline!" His hands cut through the air with each word. "Even if it means something good happens for you. You can't do it!"

"You just think that because all your dorky novels say that. But those are science fiction. They're fake. They don't know anything about real time travel."

"You don't know that," he says. "Maybe those authors found themselves in the same situation you're in and then they wrote books about it to warn others."

I roll my eyes.

"Emma, this is serious. We have to get Marci and Donovan back together."

I fold my arms across my chest. "I don't want to."

"Oh, my god," he says, exhaling in frustration. He grabs socks from his top dresser drawer and tugs a Magic Mark's baseball cap over his unruly hair, not even bothering to straighten it.

"I have to get to work," he says, ducking back into his closet and pulling another work shirt off a hanger. He shoves it in my arms. "Get dressed. We have to preserve whatever is left of the time continuum."

Chapter Nine

Wednesdays are pizza days at the Pine Grove Preparatory private school. Magic Mark's Pizza has a standing order of twelve extra-large pizzas—half cheese, half pepperoni—and Uncle Ray won't let me so much as drop a ball of pizza dough through the cool machine that flattens it into a circle.

"Just stand there and don't touch anything," he says, zooming around me in the small kitchen space while he works to prep a dozen pizzas at once.

"I can sprinkle the cheese," I offer.

He drops a circle of dough onto each metal pizza pan. "No."

"What if I fold the boxes?"

He looks like he might actually say yes, but then he shakes his head. "Don't do anything. I have to make these pizzas just like I do every Wednesday. I have to keep living my life as if you never showed up."

"But if the universe sent me here on purpose, then it knows your routine will be messed up, so we don't have to worry."

"We don't know that the universe sent you here on purpose." He reaches for a ladle of marinara sauce and expertly circles it onto the dough. "In all probability, the universe doesn't know you're here. It's too vast to care about one human's misadventures."

I frown, reluctantly recognizing the lost cause before me. Slinking back to the small office, I drop into the chair and lay my head on my hands, awaiting the boredom that comes with sitting here doing nothing. It's warm back here in the cramped office that's downwind of the pizza ovens. Everything smells like pizza, but not exactly in an appetizing way. It's like warm bread and grease and onions with every breath.

The steady hum of the massive vent hood reminds me of road noise from a long car ride, like our yearly trips to Comicpalooza in Houston, or that one time freshman year when my family thought it would be a great idea to pile into two SUVs and drive 1500 miles to San Diego for Comic Con, so that all their cosplay weapons wouldn't get held up in airport security. It took us two days of driving, and I slept so much out of boredom that I was basically jet-lagged when we finally arrived.

Nina and Addy came with us. My best friend was the Tina Belcher to my Louise Belcher. Addy insisted on dressing up like Tammy with the character's side ponytail and overdone lipstick. We took so many pictures with countless Bob's Burgers fans that weekend. It was a perfect Comic Con. But even with so much time spent together as a trio, Nina and I were still best friends. Addy often complained of feeling left out and we swore she was a part of the group, but even back then I knew it wasn't really true. There's just too much history between Nina and me to incorporate a third friend in the same capacity.

I used to feel guilty about it. But now, as I close my eyes and relive that vacation, I remember all the crush talk the three of us shared late at night in our hotel room that connected to my parents' room. Nina and Addy made fun of me merciless over my feelings for Jonah. I was basically Tina Belcher level of boy crazy, but just for him. Addy knew how much Jonah meant to me.

I don't feel guilty about anything now.

"Wake up," Ray says, some unknown amount of time later. As I blink awake, I feel like it could have been five seconds or five hours. Sitting up, my sweaty cheek peels away from my arm. I doubt I slept more than an hour at a time last night and it's all catching back up with me now. Ray sits on the desk, dusting his hands off on a cloth towel that he tosses over his shoulder. Wisps of sweaty, curly hair cling to his forehead in a sharp contrast from how his hair usually looks after half an hour with the flat iron.

"The lunch rush is over," he says. "Now we have to fix what you so royally screwed up."

"Don't put this on me," I snap.

"Whoa, what's with the hostility, Sleeping Beauty?"

I rub the feeling back into my cheek. "I didn't ask to go back in time. I didn't ask you to leave me alone for half an hour when Marci's freakin' pizza was ready. If *you* had been here doing *your* job, then this wouldn't have happened."

His bottom lip quivers and his jaw stiffens. "You're right. That's on me. But we still have to fix this."

"Why."

"Because you accidentally messed up the future, Emma. I'm sorry, but we have to fix it."

I take a deep breath. "What if I don't want to save Addy's life?"

"Are you serious?"

"Look, I've already rationalized it in my head … it's not murder if the person just doesn't exist."

"Maybe it's not the official legal definition of murder, but it's still the butterfly effect. This one tiny change could change a billion other things."

"Yeah, like make my life better."

He shakes his head. "You don't know that, Emma."

"My phone is proof that everything is better without her. I really think this is what the universe wanted me to do."

He rocks back on his heels. "And how does the universe plan to get you back to your time?"

"Er… I don't know."

He leans against the walk-in fridge, folding his arms over his chest. "It's too dangerous to think you know what the universe wants. We should at least try to fix what you messed up. If we get them back together and your phone doesn't go back to how it used to be, then I'll concede and agree that maybe you're right, and maybe you can change things all willy-nilly to suit your personal agenda."

"I don't totally love your tone right now," I say, peering at him through narrowed eyes.

He gives me a sardonic grin. "If we get Marci and Donovan back together and your phone does go back to normal then clearly you aren't supposed to be messing with the time continuum."

"Fine," I say, throwing up my arms in defeat. "Text Donovan and tell him he should get back with Marci."

Ray snorts. "That dude and I are not friends."

"What about Marci?"

He shakes his head. "They run with the prep crowd. I am solidly in the punk crowd. Trust me, these groups do not mix often."

I roll my eyes. Cliques exist in my high school, but we're not as severely divided as he makes them sound. I get along with just about everyone, plus my entire grade has been a part of the Class of 2025 group Snapchat since junior high. "So how are we going to get them back together?"

"Donovan used to work at the music store," he says, leaning out of the office and glancing out the windows toward Sam's Music. "I don't know much else about him. He graduated before I did."

The phone rings. Ray jogs out to answer it, while I linger in the hallway just out of sight of the door, should any customers come inside. He jots down the customer's order. "Seven large pepperonis!" he says after hanging up the phone. "This is going to take a while."

"I can help you?"

He shakes his head. "I wish you could, but I can't risk it."

I groan, following him around a wall of refrigerators and into the kitchen. "I wish I had my phone to keep me company."

"Who are you going to call?" he snorts, grabbing an apron off the wall hook and tying it around his waist. "None of your friends have been born yet."

I use my phone for calling people like one percent of the time, but I don't tell him that. He'll find out soon enough that phones become a constant source of entertainment, one that could help me pass the boring hours here in the back of Magic Mark's Pizza. I flip through the same magazine I read yesterday, wishing there was something else I could do, some way of getting Ray off my back about Addy so I can finally go back to my own timeline.

I find a phone book in the owner's desk and look up Addy's last name. Only there are a hundred Deblois here and I have no idea which one belongs to Donovan's parents. Plus, there's not a phone back here so I can't even try calling each number. Defeated, I spin around in the office chair.

More orders come in and Uncle Ray is busy running from the kitchen area to the phone and cash register and back again. He still refuses my offer to help him make pizzas, and me sitting here bored while he works his butt off feels wrong. Then something occurs to me. If Donovan used to work at the music store next door, maybe the current employees have his phone number.

I could call him and pretend to be one of Marci's friends and tell him she's really sad they're broken up. I can gently encourage him to go beg for her back, and maybe it'll work.

I could fix the time continuum before Ray even knows I've left.

Walking out of the office, I peek around the corner and see him busy making pizzas. Then I check the front part of the restaurant, which is empty. Now is the perfect time. Sneaking over to the doors, I grab the bells, holding them still as I quietly slip outside, letting the door softly close behind me.

Being outside feels like a rush. The warm summer air in my lungs, the big open space in front of me. I'm giddy as I rush down to Sam's Music. It's three times the size of the pizza place, with Nirvana playing from overhead speakers. Rows and rows of CDs stretch on forever. A sign on the far wall declares a long row of headphones as a "listening station". A few people mull around, headphones on their ears while they check out CDs.

This place is incredible.

I walk over to the checkout counter trying to look like a teenager who totally belongs in the year 2004. I'm once again wearing a borrowed pizza shirt and my leggings which Ray washed for me last night, and a pair of Mom's Converse. I feel like I blend in.

"Hi," I say to the back of the guy who works here. He turns around, a roll of sale stickers under one arm and a pen in his mouth. He's a huge hulking guy with arm muscles that look like they're about to burst out of his Sam's Music polo shirt. His name tag says Brent. This is the same guy I caught Uncle Ray staring at yesterday.

"Hi, sorry," he says, dropping the pen and smiling at me. "What can I do for you?"

"You have so many muscles." I don't even know why I say that, but now my cheeks flood with red hot humiliation.

He snorts. "Thanks? My dad and I have a ballin' fitness routine. He wants me to go pro."

"Football?" I guess.

He nods, but his heart isn't in it.

"Not a fan of football?"

"I love football, but I'd rather study music in college." He leans forward conspiratorially. "Which is why I'm going to Cornell in the fall with or without his permission."

"Wow," I say, realizing exactly why my uncle likes him. "Good for you."

"So what can I help you with today?"

"I heard that Donovan used to work here? Do you have his number?"

His head tilts. "I'm not sure that's a good idea."

"Why?"

He doesn't quite meet my gaze when he says, "No offense, but a lot of girls come around asking for his number. I can't just be giving it out to everyone."

"I'm not a stalker," I say, in a way that doesn't seem very believable. "I just have something really important to tell him."

Brent quirks a bushy eyebrow. "Sorry, but no."

"Do you know where he works now?"

"He spends his summers at the beach," Brent says, peeling off a sale sticker and applying it to one of the CDs in front of him. "I'm not sure which party he'll be at tonight, but he's always at one of them."

Brent's rigid stance loosens a bit as his gaze goes somewhere behind me. I turn to find my uncle standing there looking pissed.

Or relieved?

It's hard to tell with his hair in his eyes and his Magic Mark's Pizza hat covering his eyebrows. He marches up to me, touching my arm. "What the hell are you doing here?" he hisses just quiet enough for me to hear.

"Sorry," I say, turning to Brent. "I was just trying to find out where Donovan was because of that important family thing I need to tell him."

Ray's nostrils flare.

"Hey, Raymond," Brent says, flashing a toothy grin toward my uncle.

Ray's neck flushes a shade darker. He nods once to Brent then turns to me. "We have to go."

Once we're outside, my uncle sighs.

"Dammit, Emma," he says, kicking a rock down the sidewalk. "God damn, you scared the shit out of me."

"Why?"

"I couldn't find you and I started thinking maybe the time travel portal followed you and swallowed you up or something. Then I thought maybe you got kidnapped—I don't know!" He grabs his shoulders and squeezes. "Holy shit. I'm so glad you're okay. But you can't do that! You can't just go talk to people. You've already screwed up the timeline once, you can't do it again!"

"I'm sorry," I say as he shuttles me into the pizza shop and back into the office. "But I found out that Donovan will be at the beach tonight. So we have a place to look so we can find him and get him back with Marci."

I have a sudden memory of Addyson's family beach house. It's two stories tall, set up high on wooden beams that protect it from flooding and hurricanes. It's her dad's pride and joy. They spend every summer on the beach, which is a couple hours away from Cypress. I used to go there with her when we were kids, sometimes in group slumber parties and sometimes just the two of us when Nina was away visiting her abuela in San Juan.

Addyson spent years as a part of our friend group, the tertiary friend who wasn't quite part of the bond Nina and I have, but still part of our friend group. Clearly, the evidence on my phone proves that without Addy in the picture, Nina and I would still be best friends. That's *true* friendship. That's ride or die, never stab you in the back and steal your job and boyfriend friendship. Nina is a true friend. Addy is not.

Even if Ray forces me to get Marci and Donovan back together, at least I can rest peacefully knowing that Nina will always have my back even when Addy is born and grows up and ruins my life all over again.

"Seriously," Ray says, moving so that his eyes are right in front of mine. I realize he's been lecturing me about the timeline this whole time. "You can't do anything else like that. Never leave without telling me! I almost had a heart attack."

"Okay," I say, holding up my hands in surrender. "Now I have something more important to talk about."

"What?"

"That Brent guy is going to Cornell, huh?"

"Shut up."

"And you're going to Cornell." I wiggle my eyebrows.

He rolls his eyes. "I said shut up."

Chapter Ten

Now that my gigantic, idiotic mouth has screwed up and told Ray about Addy's disappearing act on my phone, I know there's no way he'll let me go back to my time without fixing her parents' relationship. I love my uncle, but he's been too brainwashed from a lifetime of reading science fiction. He lets every superstition dig into his brain and live there rent-free, making him fear things that don't even matter. When we were renovating our motel, he refused to have a room thirteen. So now, we have rooms 1-12 and 14-24. Except room fourteen is actually the previous room thirteen and everyone knows it.

The thing with my uncle is that following superstitions only changes the way *you* think about the supposed omen of bad luck. The bad luck is still there if it wants to be there. I don't believe in any of that. Luck. Omens. Butterfly Effects. They're all just made up words that humans use to explain things they don't understand.

My uncle thinks the Universe, in all her infinite wisdom, has somehow sent me back in time and expects me to make sure I don't do anything that will change the future. I know I'll never be able to get back to my time without his help—science nerds are helpful in many ways, even if they are annoying—so I guess I have to play along.

But I don't think this has to be an all or nothing situation. I think about my predicament the whole drive back home, accidentally not hearing a word Ray says about Magic Mark's annoying repeat customer named Leafy.

Here's the deal:

If Marci and Donovan break up, they never have

Addy, and my life is perfect.

But, if Marci and Donovan get back together and have Addy (as Ray thinks the Universe wants), that doesn't mean my life is still awful. I just have to change one thing that led to Jonah falling for Addy. I have to find something here in this timeline that I can change ever so slightly so that the only effect it has on the future is preventing Addy and Jonah from getting together.

How hard can that be? I've already time traveled, and honestly, that feels like the hardest part.

"The best way to find Donovan and Marci is to scope out their Myspace," Ray says as we head into the kitchen once we're back home. "Will you boot up the computer while I make a snack?"

My grandparents won't be home for another hour, so we've got full run of the house. It's hard to focus on the task at hand when I'm too busy snooping around in awe. Granny has done a total one-eighty renovation to the house over the years. New floors, new paint, new furniture. Everything still feels like home here, so I guess it's not the stuff inside the walls but the people who live there that make something a home.

The computer turns on by flipping a switch in the back of the massive CPU. Then you push a button up front. Then you turn on the monitor. Then … you wait.

I'm fascinated and annoyed by the entire process. It's like a ten minute routine just to get online.

"You ever had poor man's nachos?" Ray calls out from the kitchen.

"Pshh," I call back. "That's a delicacy in my time. But we're the only people who call it that."

While the computer does its thing, I join Ray in the kitchen. He lays out two paper plates, a bag of tortilla chips, and shredded cheddar cheese.

"Lindsey invented the name," he says, spreading

out a layer of tortilla chips on the plates.

"No, no, no," I say, nudging him out of the way with my hip. "You're doing it all wrong."

"I invented this delicacy." He puts an offended hand over his chest. "How can I possibly do it wrong?"

"The process has been refined over time, my dear uncle."

I open a couple cabinets until I find the one with real plates and then I transfer the chips. "You know when you microwave it, the cheese sticks to the paper plate?"

"Yeah…"

"With real plates, the cheese just slides right off. That way you don't waste any of the deliciousness."

He snorts. "Good idea."

"There's more," I say, ducking into the pantry. If I know my grandma—and I do—she'll have black olives, jalapenos, and sour cream. I stack all the ingredients on the table.

"Damn, Emma. These poor man's nachos are movin' on up."

"Yes, sir," I say. For most of my childhood, the infamous nachos were made by microwaving a ton of shredded cheddar cheese on top of chips. It only takes 45 seconds and is still delicious, even if "real" nachos should be made with pico and queso melted the old-fashioned way—over a stove or in the slow cooker.

But a few years ago, Nina and I got creative. Now, with the same amount of microwave time, you can have *deluxe* poor man's nachos.

Nachos in hand, we sit at the family computer and I watch, fascinated, as Uncle Ray pulls up the one and only Myspace.com. It's incredible. I've heard stories of the first social media giant, but I've never actually seen it before.

Uncle Ray's profile picture is of him dressed as

Darth Vader, which is extremely on-brand. He has 47 friends and two new messages. I'm dying to go through every inch of his page just to satisfy my curiosity of what life was like in this time, but we're on a mission.

He types Donovan Deblois into the search bar and the man we're looking for is the top result. His profile picture is exactly what you'd think it would be—shirtless, tanned, flexing, and flashing a grin to the camera.

I roll my eyes.

"It feels wrong to set up a nice lady like Marci with this dude," I mutter.

Ray snorts. "He's such a jackass. And not in a good way like Bam Margera."

This is the second time I've heard that name. "Who is that?"

"It's kind of hard to explain," Ray says, scrolling down the website. "These guys on MTV got famous for making videos of themselves doing stupid shit. It's called Jackass. Bam is like, one of the more popular jackasses. He's Donovan's idol. Donovan got his own camcorder and has been trying to film himself doing dangerous stunts around town. A couple weeks ago, he almost got arrested for shutting down Main Street to pull off a stunt."

"Tell me again why we're setting him up with Marci?"

"The Universe wants it." He clicks on Donovan's face. "This is a new picture … it might be taken where he's staying this summer."

Another page loads. "Ugh," Ray says, shaking his head. "Of course all ten photos on his Myspace are of himself. Like it would kill him to post something without his fugly grill on it."

"*All* ten photos?"

"Yeah, that's how many you can have. Let me

guess, in your time you can upload like, a hundred photos?"

I consider it for a moment. "I don't think there is a limit."

"Wow," he says, turning back to the computer screen. "Maybe I should invest in Myspace stock."

"Maybe not."

He snorts, casting a side-eyed look my way. "Let's just stop for a minute and appreciate how freaking weird it is that you're here."

"I haven't stopped thinking about that," I say. "I keep thinking I'm in a dream I can't wake up from. But I'm a light sleeper, and besides, my brain would never be this creative, which means I definitely time traveled and now I don't know how to get back."

"Look, maybe the portal didn't take you back to your time the first night because you had talked to Marci and broke the time continuum." Ray's eyes gaze off into the distance while he thinks, his bottom lip curling under his teeth. "Maybe once we get them back together, the rift in the time continuum will be fixed, and you can go to sleep again and see if it puts you back in your time."

"I have no other ideas," I say with a shrug, looking back at the tiny, slightly rounded computer screen. "Let's do this."

Old school social media is worlds different than what we have now, probably because 2004 computers were slow and internet was slower. I can't imagine trying to upload a TikTok video on this kind of slow internet. It would be impossible. Plus, my uncle's Nokia RZR is cute and all, but all it does is text, make calls, and take crappy little photos.

Despite its vintage flaws, Myspace still gives us what we need. We're able to deduce that Donovan will be at Brady McIntyre's beach house this week. Marci's profile is covered in Paris Hilton pictures and inspirational, diva-esque quotes, but once I recover from the hilariously tacky colors and pink pixelated gifs that flash nonstop, we find a post someone made to her wall last night.

It asks if she'll be at Brady's tonight, and she replied yes.

"That was ten minutes ago," Ray says, pointing at the timestamp on his screen. "Thank you, Universe, for finally giving us something good."

"Hey, now," I say, playfully smacking him on the arm. "The Universe gave you me, and I'm awesome."

"I'm sure you are awesome enough in the future where you belong," he says, logging off the internet.

Back in Ray's bedroom, I unearth my phone from its hiding place and look through it. Everything is still the same. Sweet, loving Jonah in my text messages. Addy, not existing. After tonight, if Jonah's texts go back to how they were when I arrived, then I'll know I fixed things. Then I'll start figuring out a different way to get my boyfriend back.

"You have to keep that thing hidden," Ray says, closing his bedroom door. "My parents will be home any minute. They can't see it."

"I know, I know," I say, peering at Mom's face on my wallpaper. My heart twinges a bit and I put the phone away. If I really am dreaming, this is the worst thing my brain has ever done to me. It's crueler than my recurring nightmare that I've shown up to school in my underwear and unshaven legs.

"So we know where they'll be, but there's still a problem," Ray says, pulling off his work shirt and smelling the white tank underneath. He grimaces. "I need a shower."

"Let me guess—this Brady guy is super popular

and you can't just show up to his party?"

Ray throws his smelly work shirt at me. "Nah, Brady is friends with everyone. He won't care if we randomly show up, plus he'll probably be too drunk to notice anyway."

"So what's the problem?"

"The Universe needs you to get them back together, not me. But you really can't be seen at this party because everyone who sees you is a potential time rift just waiting to happen. You can't talk to anyone else except Marci, because you've already messed up the timeline through her."

"Fine, I won't talk to anyone else."

He sighs. "It's not that easy. You can't be seen by anyone. You can't bump into anyone. It's like that Butterfly Effect movie—any tiny little change can branch off and effect every single thing in the world."

"You're giving way too much credit to some silly Ashton Kutcher movie."

"It's not just a movie. The theory has been around for decades. We talked about it in my AP bio class. One tiny butterfly flaps its wings and boom—the whole atmosphere changes."

I snort. "That's dumb. Most things don't matter."

I grab a nearby textbook off his desk and hold it up. "I could throw this book across the room and it won't matter. I could sit on it, or roll my eyes at it, and it won't matter. But I could set it on fire and throw it into the neighbor's house and that would matter, because their house would burn to the ground."

"What is your point?"

"Some things matter." I drop the book back on his desk. "Some just don't."

He disappears into his closet, returning with a black shirt and a pair of jeans. "Just sit here and don't touch anything. Don't burn any houses down. Don't do anything. I'm gonna shower real fast and then we have a timeline to fix."

I plop down on the bed. "You are so much more uptight than thirty-eight-year-old Ray."

"And you are delightfully stubborn."

I grin. "It runs in my family."

Chapter Eleven

The Gulf of Mexico isn't a glamorous beach, with its dirty brown water and lack of surfing-quality waves, but it's our beach. My family takes several trips to the coast each summer, and some years when the motel has done particularly well, my parents and Uncles will rent a beach house for a week or two and we all rock the beach bum lifestyle as long as possible.

The ocean hasn't changed a bit in twenty years.

I stand barefoot on the shore, my toes sinking into the warm sand as I gaze out at the ocean before me. The setting sun to my right casts a beautiful orange-red glow onto the water. Each soft wave rolling onto the shore feels like home. It reminds me that no matter the year, I am still on this massive rock that orbits in sun in a vast galaxy that's only a tiny spec of the entire universe.

I am made of stardust. I always have been, and once I'm dead and the world has moved on without me, I'll become stardust again. A warm comfort comes with this knowledge, and it envelops me the same way the sand slides over my feet with each wave, warming me to to my bones. A soft hug from a vast expanse.

I take a deep breath of salty air and close my eyes.

Beside me, my teenage uncle appears, smelling strongly of woodsy cologne and shea-butter lotion. The car keys in his hand vibrate with an anxiety that kind of ruins my chill-with-the-universe-energy. He turns to me. "We can't screw this up."

"We won't," I say, reaching for his slightly sweaty hand.

We parked in the public parking lot at the far south end of the beach, then took the long wooden bridge over an embankment to the shore. Beachfront homes dot the shoreline to either side of us, but the raging bonfire and thumps of music to the left tell us where the party is tonight.

"You have to be invisible," Ray says as we slowly make our way to the party. "Don't do anything to draw attention to yourself. Blend in, keep your head down, find Marci and tell her to get back with Donovan."

"I've got this, Master Kenobi," I say, shoving my hands into the pockets of Lindsey's denim cutoffs. I hope I'm not stuck here long enough to borrow the rest of her wardrobe. "I'll be a ghost jedi. I'll complete the mission."

"I do not appreciate your light-hearted demeanor," he says, taking a ragged breath.

Blending in should be easy. Dozens of young people mull around the beach bonfire, which appears to be made of a dozen wooden pallets stacked into a pile, and even more people hang out on the two-story beach house's double balconies.

"Ray-monddd!" some dude shouts from the first floor balcony when he sees my uncle. He's a tall, lanky white guy that I wouldn't imagine having such a deep voice. He waves his hands in wide arcs to catch Ray's attention. "Get yo ass up here, boy!"

"Shit." Ray looks at me.

"Go," I say, nodding my head toward the house. "Hesitating will only draw attention to you."

With a sigh, my uncle walks away, yelling something back to his friend that I can't hear over the roar of the hip-hop music that plays from some unknown location. With Ray gone, a tidal wave of apprehension washes over me as I realize I am alone, twenty years in the past, surrounded by strangers, with the fate of the entire universe hinging on me making sure some girl bangs her boyfriend at exactly the right time to ensure that my mortal enemy is born.

Chill out, Emma.
What could possibly go wrong?
****

I need a break. Acting invisible may be a state of mind, but my soul inhabits a very corporal body that I'm having a hard time hiding. My first plan—walking along the beach parallel to the beach house over and over again, secretly hoping I'll see Marci outside—hasn't gone too well. And after about ten laps, some drunken guy asked if I was lost.

I'm longing to ditch my mission and go feel the ocean splash across my toes, but there are too many people out there, too many chances to bump into someone or trip and fall and change the time continuum. Too many metaphorical butterflies, all with wings just waiting to be flapped.

So I turn my back to the ocean and walk toward the house instead. It's up on wooden piers, with parking and picnic tables underneath. A wooden shed lies just beyond the house, dimly lit by a single streetlight nearby. I walk toward it, hoping to sit on the grass and hide away from everyone for a bit.

As I round the corner, I notice two figures have claimed the hiding spot first. But they're not sitting on their butts, trying to take a break from the universal chaos they accidentally created. Nope, they're making out.

I stop short and start to turn around, but then I recognize one of the figures. Then I recognize the other one. It's my uncle, wrapped in the massive arms of the hunky music store version of the Hulk.

My jaw hits the sand. Well, maybe not really, but it's open and I taste salt in the air while a giddy little zap of joy shocks my senses. Ray finally got to hook up with his crush. Or maybe they've already hooked up before? Granny did say he'd been acting happier lately. I don't know, but I'm thrilled for him. I know this Brent guy doesn't end up being Ray's soul mate because that's my Uncle Charlie's job, but still. Maybe Brent is the reason Ray goes to Cornell in the first place.

Go Uncle Ray! Music store dude is totally hot!

I back away having done such a great job of being invisible that they don't even notice my intrusion on their secret make out spot. Reminding myself of tonight's mission, I realize the inevitable has to happen, and it might as well happen now—I have to go inside the house. Marci isn't outside and I'm just wasting time hanging out here hoping to run into her.

One time during sophomore year, Nina and I decided to ditch school so we could take a bus to the mall and wait in line for the new release of a limited-edition pair of slides that Nina had saved up months to buy. Only seniors are allowed to leave campus for lunch, and I was positive we wouldn't be able to sneak past the teacher who monitored the exit. Nina said all we had to do was act like we belonged. She said the teachers looked for kids who were nervous or acting shady, and that all we had to do was pretend that going off campus for lunch was part of our everyday routine.

It worked. And Nina got her slides, which she then never wore because she wanted to preserve their newness. If Nina ever has children, they're going to inherit a crap ton of unworn shoes.

With Nina's secret sleuthing in mind, I school my face to look neutral as I walk up the outdoor staircase to the balcony. Shuffling through groups of people, I let myself inside, trying to scope out the place without looking obvious. The kitchen floor has a dozen open ice chests filled with ice and beer. Pizza boxes and chip bags litter the dining table. Drunk, happy, dancing bodies pack the living room, and it's basically just what you'd expect of a house party, only no one is taking selfies with their phones.

Of course, I don't think that kind of thing exists in 2004.

I grab a can of Bud Light and crack open the top, taking one sip so it doesn't spill over my hand while I meander around the party, thinking the words *be invisible, be invisible, be invisible.*

"Hey, gorgeous."

I don't realize Donovan is talking to me until he steps right in my face. In a hilarious act of nature, Donovan's shirt says Jackass. I'm guessing it's a logo of the TV show he loves, but still. Spot on.

He winks, eyes dropping down to my feet and back. "I dig alternative chicks."

This is Cypress's future city councilman? A sloppy drunk college sophomore hitting on a minor? Ugh. I'm from the future and even I find this hard to believe. In my time, Mr. Donny Deblois makes himself out to be such an upstanding advocate for the city.

I give him my best WTF face. "Aren't you dating Marci?"

"No." He takes a slurping sip of his beer. "Bitch dumped me."

"She still likes you," I say, inching backward each time he gets a little closer. "She loves you."

He snorts, nodding at some dude in hot pink board shorts as he walks by before fixing his glassy eyes back on me. "If she loved me, she'd be with me right now."

"Maybe she's waiting on you to win her back."

He tips his head back and takes another long swig from his beer. "Maybe you should hook up with me to make her jealous."

I hold out my hand, which collides with his chest as he leans toward me. "I'm seventeen."

He jolts, face contorting into disgust for a fraction of a second. "Shit, I'm sorry. I don't play with underage chicks." He takes a step backward, pointing a finger at me from the hand that's holding his beer. "You come find me next year, okay?"

I grab his arm. "Do the right thing and ask for your girlfriend to take you back."

"Nah," he says, looking past me. I follow his gaze and finally see the girl I've been looking for all night, wearing a pink bikini top and white shorts. Sitting in some other guy's lap.

Donovan's cheeks cave in, then he looks away. "She can come to me."

"Fine," I say. "Have it your way."

I meander through the crowd, stopping in front of the couch. "Hi, Marci."

She doesn't hear me over the music. Her long wave of blonde hair hides her face as she listens to whatever pathetic sweet nothings this dude is whispering into her ear.

I nudge her pink high heels with my foot. "Marci."

Her head snaps up, mean-girl-scowl on her lips until she recognizes me. "Free pizza girl!" she says, beaming. "What's up?"

"Can I talk to you privately?"

"Sure." She disentangles herself from her new man and follows me into the beach-themed hallway, which is the only part of the house not packed with people. In a place that smells like beer, salt, and sweat, Marci smells like cotton candy.

"So ... I was just talking to Donovan, and he really loves you and he misses you. He wants you back."

"Of course he does," she says like this is old news. "I'm the best thing that ever happened to him."

"I think he's ready to change and be a good boyfriend."

"Are you telling me to get back with that skeeze?"

Everything in my body says no. But the universe—according to my uncle—says yes.

I bite back my thoughts and nod. "Mmhmm."

"No way," she says, glancing at her nails. Acrylic with white tips. "Donovan has been macking on every girl here all night. He's over me by now."

"He's not," I say, shaking my head. "He really, truly loves you. He's just hoping you'll get jealous and come back to him."

"Yeah, well, that's what I've been trying to do with Juan over there and it doesn't seem to matter how much I grope him or suck his face, Donovan doesn't care."

"Oh, my *god*," I groan, tipping my head back. "You're being so childish! Just go talk to him!"

"Sorry, but no. Thanks for the free pizza, though!" She flashes me a perfect smile, squeezes me into a short hug, and then disappears in the crowd.

I set my untouched beer on a nearby end table, then think twice about leaving evidence that I exist in the year 2004 and pick it back up, ducking into the crowd to chase after Marci. But she's not on the couch, and neither is that guy she was sucking face with. As I stand here in a random dude's living room looking around frantically, I realize Donovan is gone, too.

Shit.

You know what? I don't feel bad for encouraging her to get back with her loser boyfriend. Maybe they are meant for each other. They sure seem like they deserve each other, and in the future, they certainly seem happy. Now I just need these drunk idiots to realize that they are soul mates. Universe? If you could help me out, that'd be great.

Chapter Twelve

The weird thing about dreams is they can give you nightmares for no reason. Like the time I was in first grade and kept waking up thinking aliens were going to abduct me and make me live in a zoo made of humans on some terrifying alien world. My parents had to buy me a nightlight just so I could feel safer, but then I worried the light would enable the aliens to see me better, so I kept it off.

Lately, however, my dreams are normal. On my third night in 2004, I have yet another vague dream that I'm sitting in history class, barely paying attention to Mr. Colston's lecture because I'm texting Jonah. I dream of movie popcorn and cleaning the motel rooms after our guests check out. It's all so mundane in my subconscious, the normalness of everything only blurring into abnormal when I wake up in Ray's top bunk.

The ceiling is different than I'm used to. The feel of the sheets. The chill in the air. Waking up in 2004 doesn't feel like waking up at all. It's not my bedroom, it's not my real life. I close my eyes, willing that history lecture to come back, desperate for a sense of normalcy again, even if it is just a dream. I keep this up for at least half an hour, but it's not working. I'm awake.

I'm stuck in 2004.

Maybe my dreams are normal because reality isn't.

Emma Fitzgerald living and breathing in a world that's set three years before I'm even born is not normal. Real life is the dream right now, yet I can't seem to wake up from it.

"You awake?" Ray whispers from the bottom bunk. I slept on the top bunk since my mom came home late last night to crash in her own bed. It took me hours to fall asleep because I was a little worried I'd time travel back home and wake up five feet off the floor in Uncle Ray's old bedroom which is just a resting place for Granny's junk right now. Fears of my body being speared by an old coat rack in Granny's 2024 house made it hard to sleep.

But here I am, awake in the year 2004.

"Yes."

The metal bed frame creaks, then I hear Ray's feet hit the floor. He's silent for a long moment, so I roll over to the edge of my mattress and peer down at him. He's sitting up, head in his hands. His dark hair wavy from sleep.

"What's wrong?"

"Oh, I'm just on the verge of collapsing into a panic attack so severe it'll make me shrivel up and combust into a black hole."

"Why?" I sling my feet over the edge and drop down to sit next to him. "Is it B—" I stop myself before saying *Brent*, since he doesn't know I saw them last night. "Boy trouble?"

"What? No." He flinches. "It's *you*, Emma. It's *you* trouble."

I frown. "Did I snore or something?"

He sighs so heavily it can probably be heard way out in space by the very black holes he's afraid of turning into. He stands up. "We royally screwed up last night, Emma."

"Oh." I look down at my dangling feet. "Right."

For a long moment, I think he's staring off into space, but then I realize he's staring at his bookshelf where my phone is hidden under some sci-fi novels.

"Every single second you spend in the wrong timeline is a risk that you'll ruin everything. Everything you touch and eat, and everyone who sees you—it's all connected!"

"I know," I murmur, but he's not listening.

He whirls to look at me. "You can't be here much longer or the whole world might implode."

He drags his hands through his hair and groans the low, exhausted way I've heard him groan when things go wrong at the motel. "This is so bad. We have to fix Marci and Donovan."

"Or we should just find out how to get me back to my timeline," I say. I can't stand seeing him this upset, so jump into problem-solving mode. If the problem involved cosplay, or nachos, or how to Tetris a bunch of junk into the back of a Mini Cooper, I might be good at finding a solution. This problem is completely out of my element.

I take a deep breath and hope the next thing I say makes sense. "We've checked for portals, but what if it's something to do with the earth, not the house?"

"That is possible," Ray says, voice ticking up one hopeful octave. He paces the length of his bedroom, index finger pressed to his lips. "Could be astrological interference … star alignment … volcanic activity…" He snaps his fingers. "Maybe we should check the Mayan calendar."

"All of that sounds great, but I've already checked the moon phases from the date I left and then arrived here, for what it's worth."

"And?" The hope in his eyes ties my stomach in knots.

I frown. "Nothing."

With a quick shake of his head, he's back to pacing again. "Ley lines … we should check the ley lines."

"Okay." Even after three days of living in the past, my hand still instinctively reaches for my pocket, expecting to find my phone. Expecting to do a quick Google search of ley lines. Wow, I am addicted.

My hand closes into a fist instead. "Should we get on the computer and look them up?"

"Yeah," Ray says, glancing at the alarm clock on his nightstand. It's not even 8:00 in the morning yet. "We'll have to wait until the house is empty. If Lindsey sees us, we'll have a hard time explaining what we're doing. But that's fine because we have time."

I cock an eyebrow.

He stares at me like I should know exactly what he's talking about. "Before we can even think of sending you back in time, you have to fix your mistake."

"I already tried, and it didn't work."

"You need to try harder."

I shrug. "Maybe I shouldn't. Marci and Donovan are terrible together. And their daughter sucks."

"It doesn't matter," Ray says, nostrils flaring. "If they are together in your time, they need to be together in this time."

"Not really," I say.

"Yes, really!" he whisper-yells, which reminds me we are not alone in this house. Here I am with my family all around me and I can't hang out with them as me, their daughter and granddaughter. Time travel sucks.

I turn to my uncle, giving him a look that I hope is sweet and endearing, not petulant.

"By your own theory, the longer I stay here the more I mess up the future. So maybe we should focus on finding the time portal and getting me back home, that way I've only messed up one thing instead of several things." I paste on a trustworthy smile. "It's a good idea."

"That's a terrible idea. You have to get Marci and Donovan back together so their daughter will be born. We can't just leave this massive omission from the future."

"Is it really so bad that Addy never exists?" I've been thinking this ever since she disappeared from my phone, but saying it out loud makes me feel equal parts guilty and vindicated.

"Yes, Emma. Yes, it is bad."

"But she's an awful person. And her parents are awful people."

Ray lifts his hands in surrender. "So what? You don't get to play God, Emma. You don't get to decide that."

"Says who?" My hands slap firmly to my hips, and with every passing second I am more confident in my theory than his. "And since when do you believe in God anyway?"

He exhales through his nose. "I believe in science. And time traveling, though a weird ass form of science, is still science. You need to fix what you messed up and then hope it's enough to save the universe from a drastically altered future."

"You don't even like her in the future," I argue. "You think she's a brat, and you're still not over how she stood me up at the Honor Society banquet that year Nina was grounded and couldn't come! My uncle Ray from 2024 would probably be just fine with what's happened here."

"No, he wouldn't," Ray says, shaking his head. "No, I wouldn't. You can't just irrevocably change the future and be fine with it because it accidentally worked out in your favor."

"You don't know that!"

We are going in circles, arguing with no possible end. He won't change his mind, and I won't change mine. If I knew how to go back in time, I would do it right this second just to get away from him and go back to a life that is better than the one I left.

Ray sighs. "Check your phone. Is your friend still missing?"

"She's not my friend."

"You know what I mean!"

I pull back the books and CDs that hide my phone and unlock my home screen. Ray watches me, stiff as a board. Like he's wound up with anticipation. I know it's bratty of me, but I get a huge sense of satisfaction when I say, "She's still missing."

"Shit."

He turns and throws open his bedroom door. "I'm gonna get ready for work. You stay here and don't screw up anything else. I'll bring you some food before I leave."

"You're making me stay here all day?"

"Yes. In my room. Only go pee if my parents aren't around to see you, and don't, under any circumstances, interact with them. Or Lindsey."

I roll my eyes. The great thing about Uncle Ray is that I've grown up around him my entire life, but he's always managed to be my cool uncle. He's never taken on a parenting role with me, and he's usually the one standing beside me when I'm begging my parents to allow me to do something. How is it possible that teenage Uncle Ray has embodied a stuffy, strict parent attitude? Ugh.

He disappears into the bathroom, closing the door harder than necessary. A few seconds later, the shower turns on. I'm still kneeling by the bookshelf as a yawn overcomes me. I sink back onto my heels. I don't have the energy to crawl back into bed. Arguing with someone always ramps up my anxiety and makes my whole body feel like it's on a caffeine high. The awful feeling of fighting with my Uncle Ray will stay with me all day. I never imagined the coolest adult in my life would be such a joy-suck as a teenager.

I slump against the wall, cradling my phone between my legs as I stare at Mom's face on my lock screen. Her adult face is thinner with a slight tan, and some fine wrinkles that I never really noticed until I met my mother in this timeline. Staring at her picture while I'm in this amped up state will only make me cry, and I'm in no mood to cry. I press the side button and the screen goes black.

Mom—Lindsey—appears in the doorway, wearing a long shirt that covers her shorts. She's eating a Twizzler. "What's got his boxer-briefs in a bunch?"

For a fraction of a second, I want to burst into tears and throw myself into her arms and close my eyes and pretend she's my real mom in the year 2024 and not some uncanny non-maternal version of herself like she is now.

Swallowing the feeling, I shrug. "Nothing … he's just being insufferable."

She chuckles, making her way into the room. I am about ninety-nine percent sure the Misfits t-shirt she's wearing—all crisp and new right now—is still tossed in the back of her closet in my time, a faded, stretched out, super soft relic of her younger years.

"I heard y'all arguing and just wanted to make sure everything was okay."

A panicked ache throbs in the back of my throat. "What all did you hear?"

"Nothing specific." She reaches up and presses her finger over the loose tape that holds a poster to the wall. "Just the grumbly sound of Ray's voice when he thinks he's right about something."

I relax, but only a little. "Like I said, insufferable."

She grins. "He is the definition of insufferable when he wants to be. Then other days he's like, the coolest brother ever."

She kneels down, eyes wide as she pulls a CD from the shelf. "I didn't know he had the limited edition Rancid *Indestructible* album," she says with a grin. "I am so stealing this. Hey, what's that?"

She reaches over and takes the phone from my lap. It happens so fast, it's already in her hand before I even realize what's happening. White hot fear slices through me—if she turns on the screen she'll see a picture of herself. An older self. Not only would something like that have a chance of messing up the time continuum, Ray would most definitely kill me.

"Nothing!" I yank it from her grip and tuck it under my armpit. Being calm in the face of potential damage to the time continuum is not my strong suit, apparently.

"Whoa." She holds up her hands, still holding the pilfered CD. "Sorry. What kind of gadget is that? Like a fancy iPod?"

"Yeah," I say, nodding quickly. "It's a prototype. From Apple … headquarters. I'm not allowed to have it or show anyone, so I have to keep it a secret. Sorry."

Lindsey frowns. "How did you get it?"

"If I told you, I'd have to kill you."

"You're weird, Emma." Her lips quirk up into a grin. "But I like you."

Chapter Thirteen

I can't believe he actually means it. Uncle Ray is making me stay home today. I thought he'd be in a better mood after a hot shower, but when he emerges from the bathroom dressed for work, with hair slicker than a seal, he's more set in his resolve than ever.

"Once my parents go to work you can get snacks from the kitchen, but leave everything exactly as you found it. Don't poke around, don't do anything. Just stay in my room and watch TV. And only eat a small amount of each food so there's not a noticeable difference."

I quirk an eyebrow. It's literally impossible to not change anything while I'm here—a fact my uncle chooses to ignore when he's pushing *his must save Addyson* agenda.

"Can I use the computer?" I ask.

"No."

"But I could scope out Myspace some more and find out where Marci will be tonight."

"No. You need to see her in person, just the two of you, and fix this mess without somehow messing up even more. I don't know how to do that yet, so you stay here."

"Let me come to work with you," I say, my voice taking on a childish pleading note that makes me cringe. "We'll call her and offer her another free pizza and then I'll just recreate the first time I met her, but I'll tell her to get back with Donovan." I snap my fingers. "Easy peasy."

"How did that work out for you last night?" He snaps his fingers back at me. It's so sassy and so perfectly Uncle Ray, that I laugh.

I hate bickering. I hate arguing. But I love my

uncle Ray.

"I'm sorry," I say. "For everything. I didn't mean to time travel, and I wouldn't have talked to Marci that day if I knew it would lead to all of this."

"I know," he says. But his expression doesn't change. He wasn't kidding when he said he woke up on the verge of a panic attack. A sheen of sweat sparkles on his cheeks, and his eyes are bloodshot, rimmed with dark circles.

"I'm really sorry. You're one of my favorite people and I hate bickering like this."

"It's fine," he says flatly. "Did Lindsey leave already?"

"Yeah, her friends came to get her a few minutes ago."

"Good," he says with a nod. "The less you see her the better."

"Are you still making me stay here all day?"

"I'm sorry, but it's for the best."

****

Hours pass. The four walls of Ray's bedroom contain multitudes of books and music and comics, but I can't focus on any of them while I'm stuck here. I flip channels on his thirteen-inch TV, which is bulky like the computer monitor. The screen is so teensy and cute. TVs are flat in my time, and the one in my bedroom is massive in comparison. Flat televisions exist in this time too, but apparently they're expensive. Ray's TV has no streaming apps. It doesn't even have apps at all. Just cable TV which has *so* many commercials.

I lay on the top bunk, remote control in my hand, watching a daytime court TV show called *Judge Judy*. My brain is too worried about the future and the past and what happens next to focus on much of anything. I think about looking for the time travel portal again, but there is literally nowhere else in this house to search.

Then I think about my own body. Standing naked in Ray's bedroom (with the door closed and locked just in case, even though I'm home alone) I stare down every inch of myself in the tall mirror on the back of his door. I don't know what I'm looking for—alien markings? Some weird stitches covering up a time travel device some mad scientist inserted into my arm? I don't know. I don't find anything. And I feel hella awkward. It's just my regular body. Pale, slightly freckled, stretch marks on my hips and scarred up knees from a childhood spent playing in a motel parking lot and stargazing on the roof.

I put my borrowed clothes back on and crawl back up to the top bunk where I can stare at the ceiling to pass the time. Maybe my phone has more clues. Maybe if I read through every saved text, examine every single photo … maybe there's something there that will help me solve the mystery of how to get back home.

I close and lock Ray's door again because even though my mom is out with her friends, heading to Zombie Radio's Dallas show, and my grandparents are at work for a few more hours, I am not risking letting anyone see my futuristic cell phone.

I smile at Mom's picture, unlock the screen, and go to my texts. Jonah's texts are the same altered conversation that they've been ever since I gave Marci a free pizza and screwed up the timeline. I back out of the text chain because memories of Jonah just make my heart hurt right now, so instead, I'll look at Nina's texts.

Only Nina's texts are gone.

This can't be happening.

Sitting up straight, I go to my photos and scroll through them frantically swiping my thumb across hundreds of pictures, half of which used to feature Nina. She's not there.

My mouth dries out and panic engulfs me. I'm hyperventilating, checking my texts again and again and again, willing Nina's name to appear. She can't be gone! The universe can't do this to me.

My vision goes blurry on the edges, turning reality into a crappy filtered Instagram photo. My hand shakes so badly the phone drops to the mattress. I swear I'm trying to breathe, but I don't think I am.

I don't think I'm breathing.

I can live with Addy disappearing. But not Nina. Not my best friend in this whole world. If anyone deserves to exist—it's Nina. Not even me. But Nina.

I slide off the top bunk in such a panic that I stumble and slam to the floor, sending shooting pains up my knees and wrists. Shrugging it off, I climb to my feet, looking around frantically for the flip flops I've been borrowing from Lindsey's closet. Finding them, I shove my feet inside, fumble with the twisty lock on Ray's door, and run outside.

I make it to the end of the driveway before realizing Magic Mark's Pizza is way across town. Pine Grove may be a small town, but it's too far to walk. My eyes turn to my mom's Bimini blue 1994 Mercury Cougar. She won't need it anytime soon because she's traveling with her friends. Me driving a car—or, stealing a car if you want to get technical—twenty years in the past might be a teensy tiny little break in the time continuum. But desperate times, desperate measures, and all that.

Her car keys are on the hook by the garage door and I'm cranking up the engine before I can talk myself out of it. Ray won't be off work for two more hours and that's two hours too long. I need to get Nina back now.

Chapter Fourteen

My uncle taught me how to drive when I was fifteen. His instruction came on the heels of my mom's abrupt resignation, terror-stricken after the first time she let me behind the wheel of her car, and decided she wasn't going to teach me. I don't even think I drove bad that very first time we went out in the high school parking lot, but Mom kept slamming her foot on the floor in the passenger side, her fist gripped tightly over the handle above her. I hadn't even gone over forty miles an hour, but she claimed that was too fast for a parking lot. Apparently speed bumps shouldn't make the car lift inches off the ground.

My dad's truck is so big I felt like a bus driver, so he couldn't teach me, and Uncle Ray's Audi means more to him than just about anything, so I couldn't drive that. But my Uncle Charlie came to the rescue by loaning me his Mini Cooper, so long as Ray was the one risking his life in the passenger seat next to me. A year later, he gave the car to me for my birthday.

While everyone else had taken me to the high school parking lot, parked, swapped seats with me, and then gave me a lecture about how to buckle my seatbelt and check the mirrors before I ever started the engine, Uncle Ray just tossed me his husband's keys and said, "Let's drive."

"Where to?" I'd asked.

He just grinned and said, "Anywhere."

That's how we ended up and Granny's house, an hour away. By the time I parked in her driveway, I'd felt more confident driving than I ever had making circles around a parking lot. It was a perfect mini road trip, made even better because Granny was so happy for the unexpected visit, she made us brownies.

That memory plays through my mind while I drive to Magic Mark's Pizza, wheels on the same asphalt of the same road, at the same GPS coordinates, two decades before my memory even happened. If I don't fix the timeline, what else will change? How many of my memories will become simply fiction? Fantasies of a future that has never happened. A future that never will happen.

The world deserves to have Nina Rojas. I drive a little faster.

Magic Mark's has two entrances, although technically the one I enter into is the exit door that most people never notice because there are no stickers on it from the outside of the glass. The main door enters right into the front counter, where Ray stands at the cash register taking orders and answering phones. The other door exits from the tiny little dining room, the adjacent section of the restaurant that smells like mold and old carpet. There are only four tables here. In my short tenure into the past, I've never seen anyone sit down to eat. I figure this is the safest place to hide out until the two customers at the counter get their food and leave.

The customers standing at the cash register don't notice me enter, or maybe they just don't care. Ray notices, though. And he cares, judging by the look he flashes me which unleashes a tidal wave of anxiety through my gut.

I've never noticed the three vintage arcade games in the back corner of the dining area, but Ms. Pacman calls to me with her pixelated bright colors flashing across the screen. We have one of these at the motel. The lockbox on the front is unlocked and the game is set to free mode. I've joystick-ed my way through millions of dots in my life, securing my initials in the top ten. Never scoring higher than RAY or RSX, my two uncles' top two scores on the leaderboard.

This one requires quarters, which is yet another thing I don't have here in 2004. I stand in front of the machine, hands on the controls, watching the demo screen play out in front of me. The seconds feel like hours. Finally the customers leave and Ray appears behind me.

"You found the portal."

"Huh?" I blink, shaking my head. "No."

A muscle in his jaw twitches. "Then. Why. The hell. Are you. Here?"

"Nina's gone."

He goes still. A morbid, painful recognition flashes in his eyes and I know I don't have to explain any further.

"How did this happen?"

My voice is raspy for reasons I don't understand until tears pour out, and my throat feels like it's going to close up. "I don't know how this happened," I say, pacing a few steps forward then turning back on my heel. "I haven't talked to anyone who knows Nina's parents! She wasn't even born here, she was born in Canada. And I'm pretty sure her parents are still in the Dominican Republic right now. They haven't even immigrated here yet so how could I possibly have broken them up?"

"Deep breaths," Ray says, his hand on my shoulder. "I can't have you passing out. Because then I'll panic and pass out and then we'll both be screwed."

Despite my half-ass attempt, my lungs don't want to take a deep breath. They just want to keep hyperventilating, making the edges of my vision blur a little bit. And I'm inclined to let them because I am FREAKING OUT.

"But how did this happen?" I don't even sound

like myself anymore. I sound like some high-pitched frantic lady losing her mind in the back of a pizza place. "How did this happen? I haven't seen Nina's parents so I know I haven't broken them up. Now can she *not* be born?"

Ray's lips press together in thinking mode. "I don't think you did anything to break up Nina's parents."

"Then where is she?"

"Maybe she's just not your friend in the future. Or she never moves to Cypress…"

"No." My head shakes furiously back and forth. "That can't happen."

Ray shrugs. "Maybe you two aren't friends in the new future you've created. Maybe you're enemies."

"Oh, god." I lurch forward, putting a hand on the wall to steady myself. All the Lucky Charms cereal I ate for breakfast is about to reappear on this black and white checkered floor. The only thing that stops me from vomiting is sheer force of will. I can't allow this worst case scenario to happen.

"Nina and I would never be enemies," I say, standing up straighter, even though my stomach still clenches nervously. "That's not what happened."

"Whatever happened, it's the result of a chain reaction," Ray says.

"The butterfly effect," I mutter.

He nods. "It's the butterfly effect from the first event you caused, which was Marci and Donovan's breakup."

"I have to fix this."

"Yeah, dude." Ray's eyes widen. "That's what I've been trying to tell you. If you get them back together, it might set everything back in order. You might be able to unflap the butterfly wings."

"Might?" I say, blinking as a cold tear runs down

my cheek. I'm not crying anymore, but it must have been lingering in my eyelashes, trying to decide what my emotions will do next. *"Might?"*

Ray takes a deep breath, a look of resignation and hope mixing together under the brim of his Magic Mark's baseball cap. "We have to think outside the box here." Ray closes his eyes and breathes in. I think he's about to summon a séance or something, but then he opens his eyes and exhales, blowing a raspberry with his lips. "I've got nothing."

I burst into tears.

"Don't cry," he murmurs, patting my back. He doesn't tell me not to worry because my uncle is a straight shooter. He doesn't know if it'll be okay. I don't know if it'll be okay. I was fine with Addy not existing, thrilled even—but not Nina. I realize on the whole cosmic scale of things, that probably makes me a terrible human being.

Actually, on a cosmic scale, I don't think any of this matters. But I am not a galaxy, or a vast universe. I'm a girl. And I want my life back.

"I don't want to be here anymore. I don't want to spend the rest of my life here, or in the future if it's not with Nina. I can't do that. I have to make things right," I say through tears. I hate that I'm crying, but it's better than throwing up. My body still seems like it'd be happy doing both.

I wipe my eyes dry with the back of my hands and then stand a little straighter. Panicking is not going to cut it. Our school resource officer always says that a lack of knowing the law doesn't excuse you from breaking it. I don't have to know the details; I just have to fix this.

"It doesn't matter if we don't know how to do it," I say, drawing in a deep breath that reaches all the way to the center of my heart. "I'm going to fix Marci and

Donovan, find the time machine, and get the hell back to my best friend."

Chapter Fifteen

Determination takes over me like a thick sweater, warming my insides. There is a way back home. There is a way to fix everything. I may not know how yet, but I believe it. Believing is half the battle. Maybe my uncle is exhausted of being so stressed out all the time, but he doesn't lose his mind over my borrowing of my mom's car. I follow him back home, both of us motivated to fix the rift in the time continuum. I think my uncle has been this motivated from day one, but I've only finally caught up to him.

"Walk me through what happened the day you time traveled," Ray says, tossing his car keys on his desk. "The answer must be there somewhere. We'll find it."

I take a shuddering breath as I remember my last day in the year 2024. It was just three days ago, but it feels like a lifetime ago. Maybe because it is—it's twenty years into the future before any of this actually happens.

"I live in Cypress," I say, trying to start as far back as needed. "So does Nina. And Addy's family lives there, too. Granny still lives here in Pine Grove, in this house, obviously. And … I was coming to visit Granny for the summer, but at the last minute Nina said she's coming with me."

Ray's dark, focused eyes make him seem so much older in this moment. When I look at him, standing there, arms folded across his chest, jaw set in thought, I get chills. He's focused and attentive, a younger version of the man I know in my time. Everything still feels balanced on a thin wire between hope and hopeless, but if anyone can help me it'll be him. My steadfast, never wavering Uncle Ray.

"When did Nina decide to go with you?" he asks.

"Literally when I was about to drive away. She gave up her summer plans and everything because I was hurting and she wanted to be there for me." Another tear falls down my cheek.

"And you were hurting because of Addyson Deblois?"

I nod.

"What happened next?"

"We drove to Granny's."

"Anything unusually happen on the trip?"

I shake my head. "We got here and we dropped our stuff in Mom's old bedroom."

"Show me," he says, holding an arm out for me to go first. We go to my mom's room—a craft room slash guest room in my time, but it's young Lindsey's room now. "Show me exactly how you walked into this room on that day," he says.

I do my best to reenact the boring activity of Nina and I walking inside and dropping our bags on the bed.

"So you didn't notice any kind of time portal awakening when you walked into the room?"

I can't help but laugh, even though he's serious. "No," I say when it's clear he's waiting on an answer. "I didn't notice a time portal opening."

He sighs, disappointed. "Okay, well keep going. Walk me through the night."

"Nina and Granny thought I should go scream my anger out and that maybe it would help, so we went to the barn."

"The barn, which had the weird telescope in it?"

"Yeah," I say slowly. "That was a really weird telescope..." Chills erupt along my arms, raising the hair on my neck. they're the kind of chills you get when you can tell someone's standing behind you. Intuition?

My eyes narrow. "What if the telescope is the

time machine?"

"It's not here," Ray says, shaking his head. "My dad doesn't own it yet."

Frustration as me tugging on my scalp. "So what, we have to find a telescope before we can get Marci and Donovan back together?"

"Deep breaths," he says, holding out his hand as if that'll make my heart stop crashing against my chest. "You said the telescope did something weird. What exactly happened?"

"We were in the barn screaming at the top of our lungs, and Nina told me to stop holding my phone, so she took it and set it on a wooden stool thing that was next to the telescope. After a few minutes, the setting sunlight was streaming in through the cracks in the roof and it came in through the telescope, which almost caught my phone on fire. But it was really cool—it was pink," I say, remembering the weird event in a new light now. "I guess I didn't think much of it at the time. I was afraid my phone would be damaged, but it wasn't."

"Pink?" Ray's head cocks to the side. "What was pink? Your phone?"

"No. It was like a pink smoke zapping out of the eyepiece of that old telescope. I've never seen anything like it."

"That has to mean something. Let's check out the barn again, even though I'm pretty sure there isn't a telescope in there."

My grandparents are watching the television in the living room and playing a card game on the dining table. It's an old TV sitcom about a tool man and his family, but I can't remember the name of it.

"You kids want to play?" Joe calls out.

"Not now, sorry," Ray says. "Maybe later."

I would love to play a card game with my

grandfather, but I've seen first-hand how my very existence here is ruining the life I have in the future. Granny only has a few more years with the man she loves, and I want her to enjoy every second of it.

In the barn, Ray and I once again look through everything. There's maybe twenty percent less stuff crammed in here than in my timeline, but it all looks remarkably the same. A bunch of old junk shoved in a barn. An artificial Christmas tree. Plastic buckets of Christmas lights. One terrifyingly creepy plastic snowman.

Zero telescopes.

I can't even find the wooden stool.

"I wish we could just ask him if he has an antique telescope," I say. "But asking him might mess up the timeline."

"If he had a telescope, I think he would have mentioned it by now," Ray says. "My dad loves space. He goes to the Houston Space Center every time they have a new event going on. He and my mom go to the observatory all the time. It's where they had their first date. So if he had a telescope, I think I'd know about it. My dad freaking loves space."

"That's so cool." I grin. All these years I thought I had nothing in common with my adoptive grandparents because I didn't share any of their DNA. Turns out I was wrong. My grandfather is amazing. "I love space, too."

"Maybe the telescope is important, but maybe not," Ray says. He's all business, unaware of the sweet moment I'm having in my own mind. "Let's keep recreating the night you time traveled. What did you do after the screaming? And by the way, that's genius. I want to come out here and scream, too."

"Do it," I say, wiggling my eyebrows. Taking a deep breath, I yell out, *"Scream!"*

"Aagh," Ray bellows, opening his arms wide.

"That was good for a first-timer," I say, shrugging one shoulder. "But Nina would say you aren't putting your heart into it."

"What else happened?" he says, shoving his hands into his front pockets.

"We screamed for a while," I say. "I was angry at Jonah so I just kept picturing that each scream was somehow going from my heart into his face."

Ray rolls his eyes.

"Make fun of me all you want," I say. "It was cathartic."

I toss my head back and yell again, giving it my all as a way to impress my best friend, wherever in the universe she may be right now. Ray does the same. We yell, and yell, and yell. But instead of a high-pitched, horror movie scream, Ray's screams are low and guttural. Angry. Exhausted.

"Screw you, Donovan!"

"Whoa." I turn to Ray, my head a little dizzy from all the yelling. "Where did that come from?"

"You said it helped to think of someone you hate."

"We don't have to like Donovan, but we do have to want him to succeed in getting back with Marci."

"Yeah," he says. His brow is dotted with sweat. "Of course. I just hate him."

"Why?"

"Reasons." He shrugs. "So what did you do after you screamed out your rage in the barn?"

I take him through the rest of my evening with Nina and Granny, trying not to reveal too much about the future. I don't want him to know his dad has already passed away in my time. Recreating the night comes easily to me because those last moments in 2024, before I knew time travel was real and before everything flipped upside down, are burned into my mind. I only thought my life sucked back then.

Now it might not even exist for much longer.

"And then we went to bed," I say, several minutes later.

We're in Lindsey's room now. "I slept on this side and Nina was on the other. In my time, there are two white wicker nightstands on each side of the bed. She fell asleep quickly because she always does, but it took me a while to stop thinking about Addyson and Jonah and how much I dislike both of them."

Ray leans against the door frame, one hand resting on his chin. "Show me exactly what you did from the time you walked into this room until when you woke up in my time. Leave no detail out."

"Okay…" I mime digging through my bag and getting the leggings and shirt I slept in, then I mime changing clothes, pretending to toss my old clothes on the same spot on the floor where I left them in 2024. I pull down Lindsey's comforter and crawl into her bed.

"Of course, I had my phone because I can't sleep without it," I say, pretending to reach out to the nightstand and pick it up.

"Go get it," he says.

With my phone in my hand, I crawl back into bed. I lay down, tugging the sheets up my chest. I glance to my left, picturing Nina in all the empty space that exists now. Tears well up in my eyes again. "She's the best friend anyone could ever have."

"Every detail," Ray says. "Don't leave anything out."

I nod, looking up to the ceiling and the glow-in-the-dark stars. "Nina and I decided to get donuts as a surprise."

"At night?"

"No, in the morning. We wanted to wake up really early, so I set my alarm…" I unlock my phone and click on the clock app. I tap the alarm tab. "Wait…"

I sit up. I blink a few times, but it doesn't change the screen.

"What is it?" Ray says, peering at my phone.

"This is different."

I have two dozen alarms on my phone, half of which are set for five-minute increments starting at 6:00 in the morning so I'll wake up on time for school. They've been turned off since the first day of summer. They all have just the time. The alarm at the very top of my screen, however, has something else.

6:00 AM 2004

"What is it?" Ray says. He's so close I can smell the garlic bread we shared for dinner on his breath.

"I think I accidentally set my alarm for 6:00 in the morning in the year 2004. Which doesn't make any sense because the alarm clock app doesn't work like that. It's never had a year before. You just pick the time."

Ray frowns. "Try making a new alarm."

I tap the plus icon to add a new alarm, and sure enough, it wants me to put in a time and a year. I don't remember seeing this feature the last time I set my alarm with Nina by my side, but maybe I didn't notice it. What the hell is happening? I look up at Ray.

"If I set the alarm for 2024 and then go to sleep, you think I'll wake up in my time?"

He's quiet for several seconds, his eyes on my phone screen. "That's what it looks like."

"How?" I breathe the word.

"The telescope? The pink smoke? I think that telescope did something to your phone." Ray's hands dig into his hair, his eyes wide as a grin slides across his face, changing his boyish features into something slightly more deranged. "Emma … you found it."

"The telescope," I murmur, remembering the whimsical pink smoke, seeing it in my mind as clear as when it happened. "It was the telescope, after all."

"Maybe it shot gamma rays into your phone or something."

"Gamma rays?" I snort. "My phone is not the Incredible Hulk."

"You know what I mean!" He sits at the foot of the bed, his eyes sparkling with whimsy and a tiny bit of fear. "That telescope did something to your phone. Something molecular, something—I dunno—astrological. It *changed* your phone into something else entirely."

I look up at Ray. "This is it."

His mouth hangs open, then his eyes meet mine. "This whole time we were looking for a portal. But it's not a portal that brought you here. It was a time machine. Emma, your phone is a time machine."

Chapter Sixteen

When my phone time-traveled twenty years into the past, bringing me with it, it did not bring its own charger. Probably because I had been too lazy to fish it out of the bottom of my backpack before falling asleep that night. My phone is still fairly new and the battery life lasts for days. I hadn't charged it a day or two before I went to Granny's house. Now it's been hiding in Ray's shelf for four days, slowly draining the battery with each passing second. Like an idiot, I've left my phone on this whole time.

Now it's Friday morning, so early the sun hasn't risen yet, and I've just rocketed awake with the horrible realization that my phone's time machine qualities will only last as long as it has battery life. I hop off the top bunk and retrieve my phone.

Twenty four percent battery life.

I curse under my breath as I unlock the screen and turn the battery-saving mode on. I turn off data, GPS, wi-fi. I go into the settings and check the battery life. It estimates it has three more days of battery life left. I check my texts one more time just to verify that Nina really is gone and it wasn't some horrible dream, and then I turn off the phone.

"What's going on?" Ray says groggily as he sits up in bed. "What time is it?"

"I need a phone charger."

"Huh?" He yawns, tapping the touch-lamp on his nightstand. A soft glow fills the room.

"My phone," I say, holding it up. "The battery will only last three more days without a charger."

"You can use mine."

I roll my eyes. "That charger won't work on my

phone. Even if you had an iPhone, the charger wouldn't work because they've been updated over time."

"What's an iPhone?"

"You don't have iPhones?"

"I have an iPod. Is that what you mean?" He yawns, stretching out his arms as he sits up in bed, his MxPx t-shirt as rumpled as his hair.

I roll my eyes. "What about a wireless charger? It can be any brand and it should work."

Ray's bewildered expression tells me they don't have wireless chargers in 2004.

I take a deep breath, willing my brain to hold back the massive panic attack I feel bubbling up in my subconscious. I hand him my phone. "Do you have anything that fits this?"

His eyes narrow at the small, thin charging slot on the bottom of the phone. He quirks an eyebrow. "Definitely not."

"It's just a battery," I say. "Surely there's some way we can charge it."

"Maybe if you're an electrical engineer," Ray says, a little sarcastically. Too sarcastically. I don't think he quite gets the seriousness of the situation. He hands the phone back. "I'm not an electrical engineer. Are you?"

"Do you know anyone who is?"

He stares at me. Of course he doesn't. My uncle is not a morning person, which would be understandable in any other situation, but right now I could really go for one of his classic moods where he blows everything out of proportion and freaks out.

"What about a robotics class at the high school?"

"This is Pine Grove, Texas," he says, running his hands through his hair. "We're lucky to have a pitifully small marching band. There is no robotics class."

"What if we drove to a college and found their electrical classes?"

"First of all, it's summer so I doubt anyone is there, and secondly—" He draws his bottom lip under his teeth, slowly letting it out while he thinks. "We can't just walk up to a stranger and show them a futuristic cell phone."

I know this, of course. I brought Ray into the cone of secrecy surrounding my time travel, but we can't afford to let anyone else know what's going on. I've already lost Nina. I can't lose anything else. I can't change the past so thoroughly that there's no hope to fix my future.

I curse under my breath. My family is definitely on the cool side of the parental spectrum. My parents are tattooed and youthful and know how to social media with the best of them. My uncles are nerdy and cool and sometimes let me drink sangria poolside, as long as it's only one and I'm not going to be driving anytime soon. But I always feel weird with cursing around my family. My family curses. My friends do it. Even Granny can spit out a string of sailor words when the mood strikes. I really don't think my parents would care, but I also never do it around them.

And I just did it. I cursed in front of Ray. I said the big one, too. The one that gives you a huge endorphin boost when it snaps out of your mouth, all deep-throated and glorious and profane.

"I'm screwed," I say, dropping my head into my hands. "I'm so screwed. I'm going to be stuck here forever in this stupid timeline with so many commercials, and no good tacos, and I won't even have Nina."

Ray barks out a laugh, and I glare at him.

"This isn't funny."

"No, it's not," he says, shaking his head. His chest

rises and falls with a deep breath. "I'm sorry I laughed. But you're not screwed. Your phone will last for three more days, right? We just have to fix Marci and Donovan in three days."

"And then hope that somehow fixing the most toxic couple in Pine Grove will bring my best friend back to me."

"It will," he says. "It'll reverse the butterfly effect. Your friend will come back. That's not just wishful thinking. That's science."

I'm not entirely sure he's right about that, but I'm not going to question it. Nina would no doubt have some inspirational Instagram post to show me if she were here. It'd have some cartoon image of a person in a yoga pose, with a colorful background, and words that say something like "project your wants to the universe and trust it to provide."

I'm not going to put out negative energy into the universe just in case it is listening.

"Okay," I say, sitting up a little straighter. "Let's make a plan."

"I have good news and bad news," Ray says. "The good news is that I'm off work this weekend."

"Bad news is you have to work today," I say, glancing at the digital clock on his nightstand. He's already fifteen minutes late for his morning hair routine.

He sucks in air through his teeth. "And I promised a friend I'd hang out with them tonight."

My shoulders fall. "So today is a total waste."

"I could skip it—"

"No, you can't. You have to live your life exactly as you would have if I never came into it. Don't stress about me. Just do your thing. I feel bad that I just fell into your life and threw your entire life into chaos. Don't worry about me," I say, flashing him a smile. "I'll be fine hanging out here all day."

"You know, even if you hadn't suddenly appeared in my life, I'd still be stressed," he says, ducking into his closet to grab a work uniform.

"What else are you stressed about?" I ask.

"Just things. Cornell. Work. Things."

"And what exactly is *things*?"

He shrugs, pulling off his MxPx shirt. "Just things."

I can feel the weight of these *things*, see it in the way he carries himself, the slumped shoulders, the crease between his brows. He's younger than my Uncle Ray, but he's not exactly better off here in 2004.

"Look, you don't need to stress about any of that stuff because—"

"Nope—" He holds up a hand. "Don't tell me anything."

I sit on the bottom bunk, reliving a Groundhog Day type of situation where I sit here bored and curious and a little panicky, watching my uncle get dressed for work. I let out an exhausted sigh. "I can't just waste the day hanging out here. I need to find Marci. Do you know where she lives? Maybe I can just walk up and down the neighborhood until I happen to run into her leaving her house."

"Marci lives on a fifty-acre ranch in a gated community with half a dozen other rich white people. You can't casually run into her."

"Well, I can't just do *nothing*. My best friend's life is at stake and I have to save her."

"Fine," Ray says. "After my parents have gone to work, you can get on the computer. Stalk everyone's Myspace and see if you can find where Marci will be tonight, and when I get home we can go find her."

****

I camp out in bed watching the weirdly surreal morning news on Ray's TV until after 9:00 when I finally have the house alone. No one ever told me my grandfather liked to sing showtunes each morning. He would have loved Hamilton. Granny cried like a baby when we first watched it on Disney+, and now I'm wondering if thoughts of her husband caused the tears more than the storyline.

Once the house is quiet, I venture into the living room, eager to do some Myspace stalking on the family computer.

"Good morning."

I nearly jump out of my skin. My young grandma sits on the couch, one foot on the coffee table and a bottle of red nail polish in her hand.

"Hi." I swallow my nerves. "I was just getting a glass of water."

"You hungry? I've got some muffins in the fridge. I can heat one up for you."

"You don't have work today?"

"It's the 2024 Annual Pine Grove Town Luncheon," she says, flourishing her hands to match her words. "It's a once-a-year four-hour spectacle where all the town bigwigs sit around and congratulate themselves on keeping a small town running for another year. It's stupid, but the food is good and I pretend to be nice so my library funding doesn't get slashed."

"At least the food is good," I say. "And yes to the muffin, but I'll heat up my own. Do you want one?"

"Yes, please. Lots of butter."

I leave her to finish painting her toenails. I know exactly how much butter Granny likes in my time, and I assume it's about the same now. I cut open two blueberry muffins, toast them, then find the butter in the fridge. The plates and silverware are exactly where I expect them to be. I guess some things change a lot in twenty years, but some things don't.

"Do you have plans today?" Granny says, meeting me in the kitchen. "If not, you should be my plus-one. Joe can't come with me this year because he's on a deadline at work."

"You want me to come to the town event thing?"

She nods, taking a bite of her muffin. "It'll be fun."

"Oh." Ray is long gone at work, but I can practically feel his spirit breathing down my neck, telling me to say no. "I don't really have anything to wear."

"No worries. I have a great dress, and I bet it would fit you," she says, eyeing me. "It's simple and classic and I promise it doesn't look like some old lady owns it." Taking her muffin plate with her, she motions for me to follow her.

"You're not old," I say, following her into her bedroom. The master room walls are painted a dark hunter green that clashes terribly with the dark blue carpet. It's not even close to what her room looks like in my time. Granny's bedroom is tidy, however. That much is the same. The bed is made, the antique vanity has her perfumes and makeup neatly organized. Some of my mom's high school photography photos are framed and hung on the wall. It smells like baby powder in here, exactly the same as Granny's room back at home.

In my time, Granny's entire house is painted a light gray inside, with wooden flooring in every room, except the kitchen which has been redone with white granite counters and sleek charcoal gray cabinets. All the white appliances have been swapped out for dark stainless steel.

I stand near her bed while she disappears into the walk-in closet, emerging a few moments later with a black dress. It's sleeveless and knee-length. No frills—just simple and timeless.

"What do you think?" She holds it out to me.

"It's pretty."

Her eyes sparkle. "Go try it on."

I can't think of a good excuse to deny her request, and I also just don't want to. This is much more fun than being stuck in Ray's nerdy comic-book-loving bedroom all day. I slip into the dress, contorting my body to get the zipper pulled up all the way, and then I stare at myself in the bathroom mirror. The fabric is slightly loose in my hips and boobs, but it works.

Soon, I'm handed a pair of pink strappy sandals and a matching pink headband that Granny promises looks great in my hair even though hard headbands are not even remotely in fashion where I come from. I finish my toasted blueberry muffin slathered in butter and watch the hummingbirds on the back porch while she finishes getting dressed. It only takes a little bit of effort to shove down the guilty feelings that nag at me. She's my grandmother. I don't want to leave. But I can't change the timeline, either. I'll just have to make it work.

Granny wears a navy blue pantsuit with cream-colored high heels, her blonde hair twisted into a sleek bun. She's absolutely stunning. A confident, powerful woman. Dorothy Ross is timeless and classic.

"It's my librarian hair," she says, patting her bun once when she sees me watching her. "These idiots on the council expect their librarian to look like a librarian, and I oblige because—"

"Gotta get that funding," I say, snapping a finger-gun in her direction.

"Yes, ma'am." She winks. "You get it."

Excitement buzzes through me as we make the short drive to the community center in the middle of town. I'm filled with a nervous energy. It swirls around my ribcage and lingers over my shoulder. It's like I cheated on a test and the teacher is about to find out, and I'm just biding my time until I'm hit with detention. The more Granny talks to me, the higher my anxiety rises. I settle myself into this weird limbo where I tell her just enough of the truth to feel genuine, but I keep it vague enough to leave everything open to interpretation.

"Thanks for inviting me," I say, changing the subject when Granny asks how long I've been friends with her son. "It's way more fun coming here than hanging out in Ray's room all day."

"I take it you can't go back home?" Her expression is soft, but open. Sincere, but not pushy. I hate that she thinks I'm some kind of neglected runaway with no one who loves me at my house. It's not like that at all. In fact, I have a great life, due much in part to her and the two adopted children she raised.

I would love to sit next to her on the back porch, sipping coffee and spilling everything, but I can't risk the timeline.

I shake my head. "I can't really go home yet. I left abruptly just wearing the clothes I had on, and I've been borrowing some of Lindsey's clothes. I'll be going home soon, though, don't worry. I'm really grateful you've let me stay here."

"It's no problem at all," she says, pulling into a parking spot. "My home is a safe place. You can always come over any time you need, no questions asked."

"Thank you, Mrs. Ross."

"Call me Dot," she says. "Mrs. Ross is my mother-in-law."

I take a deep breath, steady my borrowed sandals on the cracked concrete, and try not think about how pissed my teenage uncle will be when he discovers I spent the day at a Pine Grove town luncheon.

Chapter Seventeen

I've been to the Pine Grove community center a few times, mostly to watch the county Battle of the Bands once a year with Nina and our punk rock friends and their shitty garage band music. It's an older building with tan everything from the floor to the ceiling, and even in my time, it hasn't changed much. One wall has vending machines and a long bulletin board that's littered with flyers and business cards. The other side of the room has a wooden stage that rises about a foot off the ground. It looks newer than I remember. The acoustics are terrible since the room is a rectangle. But it's the cheapest venue for garage band gigs.

The windows have white lacy curtains, the walls are wood paneling, and the whole place smells like kitchen cleaner. The last time I was here, my hand never left Jonah's. We stood right over to the left of the stage, cheering on King Ginger, who had advanced to the semi-finals in the Battle of the Bands. Nina had spent half the night talking up some college girl in the back corner of the room, only to be rejected later on when the girl realized Nina was still in high school.

I'm mildly impressed with what they've done to the place for this esteemed luncheon. Two dozen circle tables have blue tablecloths and folding chairs with white satin covers. Tea light candles flicker around the floral centerpiece, which is made of real chrysanthemums. Little nametags sit at each place setting.

A banner with the Pine Grove logo stretches across the wall behind the stage and a large wooden podium I've never seen before. A covered table on one wall features door prizes that look like random stuff donated from local shops. I spot gift cards for Magic

Mark's Pizza as well as a new vacuum cleaner and a year of free oil changes from R&B's Auto Body Shop.

Everyone is offered a door prize ticket on the way in, but I slip past the woman handing them out because getting my name drawn to win a prize might mess up the timeline. It's almost a moot point because I'm pretty sure every single breath I take here in 2004 might mess up the timeline, but I guess that's because some things matter, like breaking up a couple, and some things just don't matter, like Uncle Ray's textbooks. I'm doing the best I can here. Who knows how much the universe cares about a girl sitting in a chair at a boring luncheon in a room that smells like floor cleaner and garlic noodles in chafing dishes.

I sit at the table that has two name tags reserved for the library while Granny makes the rounds, smiling and laughing and playing the part of your local friendly librarian who definitely deserves more funding. I try to stay invisible here, too, just like at the beach party. Eyes glaze over me. Occasionally someone notices me noticing them and gives me a quick smile before looking away.

When the luncheon formally begins, everyone takes their seats. An older man in a snug tan suit takes the mic off the stage, makes everyone wince with the sharp pierce of speaker feedback, then tells us to head over to the catering table to get our food, one table at a time. Granny leans over, setting a slice of cake next to me before sitting down. I give her a quizzical look. It's not even our time to get food yet.

"Any time there's a buffet, you must get dessert first, otherwise it'll be gone after you've eaten."

I stab my fork into it and take a bite. "Noted."

The luncheon starts out just as boring as I'd anticipated, but halfway through the keynote speaker's droning speech, I notice a shock of blonde hair at a table across the room and realize the Universe just threw me a bone.

It's Marci.

She's possibly the only other person under the age of thirty attending this thing. She wears a purple spaghetti-strap sundress with a white crocheted half-cardigan over it. She's talking quietly with the woman sitting next to her who is also beautiful in that way that screams wealth, with equally white-blonde hair.

A sliver of excitement jolts through me. This is the type of coincidence that borders on magical. *Thank you, Universe! Thank you, thank you, thank you!*

When the keynote speaker mentions the town's fabulous mayor, he gestures toward Marci's table up front, to the tall, sun-weathered man sitting next to Marci and her mom.

I lean over to Granny. "Marci's dad is the mayor?"

"You didn't know that?"

I shrug. Addyson never mentioned that her grandfather was once mayor of this small town. Of course, her own dad is a city councilman and she never talked about that, either. Politics isn't exactly one of Addy's favorite pastimes.

"He's a pathetic little worm," Granny whispers. "The only thing he stands for is what he's been paid to stand for. You can have anything in this town if you have enough bribe money to win him over, which is exactly why our water bill doubled in the last year. Really makes you wonder where all that family money came from."

"Really?" I feel like I've been let in on some steamy secret. "I didn't realize small towns had corruption, too."

She holds up her wine glass for a nearby waiter to refill it. "Small towns have charm, honey, but their

THE YEARS BETWEEN US

politics are just as evil as everything else. Power corrupts people. As soon as Joe and I retire, we are out of here. We're getting an RV and traveling the country."

"That sounds fun," I say, biting back the sadness of knowing she'll never travel the country in an RV. At least not with my grandfather.

In my time, Addy's dad is a city councilman who is currently running for mayor. The town is dotted in DONOVAN DEBLOIS FOR MAYOR signs, so many that I'm pretty sure he'll win come election time. Before Addy and I had a falling out, we always talked about how we'd vote for him once we're eighteen. All of her dad's political ambitions can only happen in my time because Marci is dating Donovan in 2004.

I do the math in my head and realize that not only are they dating, but they probably get married soon because Addyson will be born in three years. At least … she should be.

Without a healthy dose of nepotism from Marci's dad, there's no way Donovan will rise to such heights in the future if he never marries Marci. Getting them back together means securing the fate of an entire town, not just the two people I know. A knot of apprehension twists itself together in my chest, pulling my spine tight and making me no longer hungry for the pasta on my plate.

Marci doesn't look over in my direction for the next two hours. I know because I'm staring at her as if my best friend's life depends on it. Walking over there myself might make me look like some kind of stalker, so I need her to notice me. There are two more hours left of this thing. I need to be patient.

Sadly, the universe gave me a time machine, but no patience. The moment Marci's chair inches backward, I'm on my feet, following her to the bathroom.

"Pizza girl!" Marci says when I meet her at the

sinks. "What are you doing at this boring thing?"

"I came with Ray's mom," I say. "She had an extra seat and I had nothing to do."

"It's boring, but the food is good," she says, flashing me a smile in the mirror while she fixes her hair. "You were wrong about Donovan, by the way."

My heart leaps into my throat. This is my chance to fix everything. "Oh?"

"He's been completely ignoring me. He even changed his AIM away message to 'single and ready to mingle'." She scowls.

I'm not even sure what that is, but I shrug it off. "He's just being immature. He'll come around. He's still crazy in love with you."

"I doubt it," she says, peering at herself in the mirror. "What are you doing after this? My parents have an afterparty of sorts after these things where everyone gets drunk and agrees to Daddy's new policies."

"That sounds awful," I say.

She laughs. "No, the fun part is that I get some friends to come hang out at my pool and we steal some booze and no one even notices because my parents are already drunk after this thing. You should come. Where's Ray? He can come, too."

"He's working until 5:00," I tell her.

"So come over as soon as you can." She boops me on the nose. I swear to god, she boops me on the nose. Just like that. Like I'm a kid or something—her index finger reached out and tapped me on the nose. She looks back at me before leaving the bathroom. "Don't forget your bathing suit, girlie."

Granny's eyes widen mischievously when I tell her Marci has invited me to her house party tonight. "I thought we didn't like her," she whispers.

"We definitely don't," I say. "But this offer just

seems too good to pass up. I thought I'd see how the other side lives, so to speak."

A waiter comes by and gives everyone a cup of coffee. I start pouring sugar into mine even though I really don't need any more energy today. My body is already hyperactive from everything that's going on.

"I can see the appeal in that," Granny says. "If you've never been in that mansion of hers, it's worth seeing."

"I just have to talk Ray into going with me."

She pats my hand, giving me a sardonic smile over the top of her coffee mug. "Good luck with that."

Chapter Eighteen

I figured there was a fifty percent chance I'd be a dead woman when Ray got home from work and discovered what happened with my day. Or maybe even a hundred percent. I don't know, I'm a high school senior, not a statistician. But when he came home, smelling a little like onions because of all the delicious ingredients that make up a pizza, the onion smell is the one that really clings to you, he went only *slightly* ballistic.

In the end, he acquiesced, noting that it's impossible to refuse his mother when she asks you to do something with her, and the fact that the clock is ticking on fixing the time continuum. No better place to fix it than at the home of the person whose future kids are in jeopardy.

A couple hours later, I find myself at Marci's house wearing a borrowed pair of my mom's lime green board shorts and matching bikini top that I'd fished out of her underwear drawer, an act that will almost definitely scar me for life.

Marci's house is the closest thing to a mansion I've ever seen in real life. It's only two stories tall, but it's a sprawling estate with marble flooring and the kind of furniture that's built to last lifetimes but no one ever sits on it. The Texas country aesthetic is strong, from the taxidermy brown bear that rears up on its hindlegs in the foyer to the hallway of creepy deer heads that leads to the game room, which leads to the pool.

All the décor is leather and wooden and Texas-shaped, with cowboy boot and horseshoe accents. When I think of cowboys, I think of dirty and rugged, worn jeans, muddy boots. Everything in Marci's estate is pristine and flawless. It's hard to picture her family riding horses, but the barn on her property supposedly has four of them, and a guy on staff who cares for them. Ray murmurs all of these fun facts into my ear as we make our way through the home after having been let in by a housekeeper. Even though Ray and Marci are in opposite high school cliques, Pine Grove is still a small town, and small town kids have known each other since kindergarten.

The Deblois family pool is awesome. It has a diving board, a slide, and even a rocky waterfall feature with a lazy river that goes around the entire thing. From where I'm lounging, it looks and feels like I'm at a resort instead of someone's private property.

I don't know what Donovan's problem is… I'd happily date Marci.

She's rich and kind of stuck up, but she's nice enough when you're alone with her. I don't know how someone as awful as Addyson ever sprung from those loins.

Music plays from built-in speakers disguised as rocks. At least a dozen younger people hang out by the pool, while well-dressed adults mull around in the house. Marci's back patio has one of those outdoor kitchen things in it, and a guy who doesn't even look old enough to legally drink is pouring a can of Red Bull and a bottle of vodka into a plastic cup.

Beside me, Ray smacks an encouraging hand on my back. "Good luck."

"Thanks."

While I'm dressed for summertime at the pool, my uncle looks like he just stumbled out of a rock show at 2:00 in the morning on the back alleys of downtown Houston. He smells a lot better than a packed nightclub, but his black Dickie's, black Zombie Radio shirt, and worn out blue Converse tell a different story. He glances out at the pool then shoves his hands in his pockets.

"What time should I pick you up?"

"What? You're not leaving."

"Yes, I am. This isn't my scene."

"No way. You're staying." I can tell he's about to say no, so I smile and wiggle my eyebrows. "Marci invited both of us. Plus," I motion toward the pool where a certain music store employee is attempting to climb on a massive pool floatie. "That guy is here."

I know his name is Brent, but I also know he was hooking up with my uncle at the beach party, and I have to play it cool so Ray doesn't figure out that I know more than he thinks I know.

"All the more reason for me to leave," he says, turning around.

I rush and stand in front of him. "I thought you liked him."

"I do, which means I need to go."

I stare at him.

He lets out a long, drawn out sigh that somehow pins a bunch of blame on me even though I haven't done anything wrong. "I'm a fat dude—I don't do swimming pools."

"You're not fat," I say.

"Well, I'm not Donovan, either."

I follow his gaze to where Marci's ex-boyfriend himself is standing at the edge of the diving board, wearing a white Speedo that leaves only one thing to the imagination. Every other inch of his tanned, muscular body is on display. Donovan yells out something idiotic, his friends cheer, and then he dives into the pool.

"Very few people are like Donovan. That doesn't make you any less worthy of going in the pool and hanging out with your friends."

He snorts. "My hair will get messed up."

"So don't go in the stupid pool," I snap. "But stay

with me, at least until I can make sure those two beautiful jerks are back together and the timeline is fixed. Then we can leave."

"Fine," he says, glancing back toward Brent as he drops onto a nearby lounge chair. "But hurry up, Cupid. You have a match to make."

Marci seems genuinely happy to see me. She even hops off her towel and abandons the two friends she'd been talking to when we arrived, choosing instead to rush over to Ray and me, a bright summery smile on her sun-kissed face.

"Hey, girlie," she says, pulling me into a quick hug. She waves a hello to Ray, then takes my hand and pulls me over to the lounge chairs next to him. "I'm glad you could make it. I tried finding you on Myspace, but I don't know your last name, so I couldn't find you."

"I don't use Myspace."

She gives me a surprised look from over the top of her sunglasses. "That's awesome sauce. You know, I keep thinking I should just delete mine and, like, live mysteriously, ya know?" She exhales whimsically, turning to look at the pool. At a specific someone in the pool, if I had to guess. "Getting rid of Myspace would save me the hassle of seeing which new girl Donovan has added as a friend lately."

"Aww, come on. You two can work things out," I say with all the confidence of someone who has seen the future.

"Nope. No, we can't." There's a hint of resignation in her voice, and I am not okay with that. She holds up her hand—a move that feels totally out of place until an older woman wearing a light blue maid's uniform appears from out of nowhere with a tray of drinks. I'm handed a glass with some kind of red fruity slushy drink that comes complete with a blue paper umbrella. It feels like I'm at a resort instead of someone's house.

Marci thanks the maid and then asks her for some chips and guacamole.

"There's no booze in this," Marci says, tipping the straw to her lips. "My mom refuses to openly serve alcohol until all of my friends are twenty-one, but you can sneak some from the fridge over there if you want."

"Thanks, but I'm good."

"Ray?" she offers.

He shakes his head. "I'm driving."

"You know what?" Marci says. "I like you guys. You're legit. You're my new straightedge friends who don't use Myspace and just live life the way they want..." She nods, more to herself than anyone else, then holds out her drink to me. "Here's to awesome new friends."

We clink glasses in a toast. I remind myself to focus on the task at hand. "Donovan really does love you," I say. "I feel so awful for telling you to break up with him."

"It is what it is." Marci shrugs. I can't see her eyes from under her sunglasses, but they're probably closed as she lies back on the lounge chair, face tipped toward the sky.

"It's obvious he still has feelings for you."

"How so?"

"He's here at your party," I say. "That has to mean he still has feelings for you."

She snorts. "There are a dozen guys here, and I'm not dating any of them, so mere presence at my party doesn't really mean anything. If anything, he's just trying to make me jealous, flashing that hot ass body all over my backyard."

As if to punctuate her point, she lowers her sunglasses and watches her ex-boyfriend flex his muscles for a crowd of admiring fans from across the pool. It seems weird at first, but then I realize one of Donovan's friends is recording his silly poses on a handheld camcorder that's the size of a football. Donovan climbs onto the diving board, flexes his muscles a few more times, then jumps into the air and does a massive belly flop into the water.

Marci rolls her eyes and shifts, angling her body to face me, not the pool. Her French-tipped acrylic nail sways from Ray to me. "You two are a cute couple, by the way. I'm digging the punk rock dude with the cool, laid-back girl vibe."

"Oh, we're not dating," I say, trying to ignore the tingle of excitement I get from Marci calling me *cool*. I guess popular girls have that effect on you no matter what timeline you're from.

"We're just friends," Ray says. "Basically family members."

He's been glancing over at the hot tub so often you'd think he's getting paid to lifeguard it. Brent sits in one corner of the hot tub, hulking body wedged in with a few of the guys wearing LSU swim shorts and half a dozen college-aged girls. I pretend I'm playing with the tiny paper umbrella in my drink cup, but really I'm sneaking glances of my uncle who is sneaking glances at Brent.

Brent's eyes find his from across the patio. He nods once, more of a chin lift than anything, but even in my time, I know the subtle chin lift is a patented "cool dude" gesture that means hello. Jonah used to head nod at me all the time when we first started dating.

Brent lifts a hand out of the water and makes the slightest motion, a barely perceptible "come join me" sign directed to Ray.

Ray's neck flushes red. He shakes his head softly.

Brent pokes out his bottom lip, a two-second flash of puppy-eyed disappointment. Then his expression goes back to normal and he's suddenly back in the world of the hot tub, a popular guy with his popular flock. Ray looks down at his phone, his Adam's apple bobbing as he swallows.

My heart aches for my uncle, but only for a little bit. His true soulmate is my Uncle Charlie, and they'll meet each other in college.

"Someone's phone is going off," Donovan says, hopping across the pool water. He hoists himself out of the pool, dries his hands on a beach towel, and grabs a phone off the patio table. He squints at it. "Bet you wish I was there instead of all those girls," he reads aloud. He looks up. "Whose phone is this?"

Beside me, Ray curses, shoving his phone into his pocket. I make the connection just a second too late, because now Donovan is scowling in disgust and holding up a small blue phone with an even smaller glowing blue screen on the front of it. "Brent, isn't this your phone?"

"Yeah," Brent says, having just now looked up from the hot tub. "Get off my phone, bro."

"*Bet you wish I was there instead of all those girls,*" Donovan says again, holding up the phone between his thumb and index finger as if it's dirty. "Who is HotBoy and why are they sending you this text? You gay or something?"

Brent's eyes widen. "Dude, leave my phone alone."

All eyes in the hot tub are now focused on them. I glance around, grateful that most of the party-goers don't even realize what's happening. Marci has left her chair to help the maid bring out a massive tray of chips and guacamole.

Donovan's brows narrow. "Dude, are you gay?"

Brent wraps both arms around the girls on either side of him. "Do I look gay?"

"Look, I don't care if you are, but I'm your best friend."

"Let it go, man," Brent says with a lighthearted chuckle.

Donovan clearly isn't ready to let anything go. "I should know these things, bro. I need to know who to set you up with because you have been single for way too long—just say the word and I'll kick these girls to the curb and get some fine ass dudes in here."

I can't tell if Donovan is joking or actually being supportive. Maybe it's a bit of both. The girls in question start objecting to the idea of being kicked out.

"Dude, I'm straight," Brent says. He chuckles, smiling at the girl to his left. "That text is an inside joke. You wouldn't get it."

Donovan drops the phone back on the table. "So, you don't prefer guys?"

"Nah, man. I'm straight as an arrow."

Donovan lowers himself into the hot tub between two other girls who seem all too happy to have him.

Marci returns, doing a little happy hip jiggle as she sets the tray down on the concrete between our chairs. "Drag your chair closer," she says, motioning toward me. "This guac is to die for, trust me. Ray, you want some?"

My uncle shakes his head. It's right about now that Marci notices Donovan and his new position as the filling in a hot tub girl sandwich. Daggers shoot out of her eyes. "I should have him escorted off the property," she mutters, reaching for a tortilla chip.

The Universe could have sent me anywhere and yet it chose to throw me in the middle of deluded young lovers who refuse to stop tearing each other down and get back together already.

Ray sits up in his chair. "I'll be in the car."

"What? No!" I reach for him, but he ducks out of the way, walking straight through a side gate in the fence that I hadn't noticed before. I jog to keep up with him as he walks down the long, winding brick driveway toward his Mustang.

"Ray, stop. Talk to me."

"It's fine, Emma."

"No, it's not fine."

I grab his hand and tug him around. Tears pool in his eyes. He looks away, his jaw tightening. "Talk to me," I say. "Just talk."

"He promised he'd come out once we graduated high school." Ray's voice wavers. He tightens his jaw again and looks out at the bright blue sky. "He promised we'd stop keeping it a secret." A tear rolls down his cheek and he roughly swipes it away with the back of his hand. "He promised."

"I'm sorry." I pull him into a hug, but he's rigid, arms held to his sides, so I let go.

"Just go make sure you accomplish what you need to get done. Don't worry about me. I'll be here waiting to drive you home."

"I'm not going anywhere." I walk over to the Mustang's passenger door and pull it open, sit down, and close the door behind me. It's swelteringly hot in here, so I hope Ray doesn't make me suffer very long.

Ray leans into the driver's side door. "What are you doing?"

"Let's go home. We'll eat ice cream and watch movies. If Nina were here, she'd have a better idea for mending your broken heart, but this is the best I've got."

"Emma…"

"I'm not letting you sit here and be sad over some

guy."

Ray slides into the driver's seat. "You only have two more days left to fix the time continuum. My broken heart doesn't matter right now."

"Yes, it does."

"You need to go back and talk to Marci."

I fold my arms over my chest and shake my head in one decisive movement.

"You only have two days left!"

"It only took me thirty seconds to break the time continuum," I say in a voice that is significantly more confident than I feel. "I can fix it in two days."

Chapter Nineteen

I wake up Saturday morning to the smell of bacon. This is the first time I know exactly where I am as I yawn awake, stretching out my limbs in the small twin-sized top bunk. I'm no longer disoriented like I was the last few days of waking up somewhere other than my own bed in my own motel home back in Cypress. I'm no longer under the delusion that maybe everything I've been through was some elaborate dream and now I'll finally wake up in my own bed in my own time. The year 2004 has given me a sort of time travel Stockholm syndrome.

I stare at the ceiling. Ray's ceiling is painted white, devoid of any personality at all, unlike Mom's ceiling in the next room over, which is covered in made up glow-in-the-dark constellations that you might find in a completely different universe, but not ours. I reach out my hand, thinking I might be able to touch the ridges in the drywall, but it's still a little bit too far away, just a few inches from my fingertips. Story of my life. Everything I want is just a little too far away.

Sliding off the top bunk, my feet thunking down on the carpet is the only sound in this empty room. Ray's bed has been made, and the clock on his nightstand tells me I slept until 10:00 in the morning. My phone is down to seventeen percent battery life and Nina is still gone. I don't even know why I checked. I didn't complete my task yesterday. I didn't get Marci back with Donovan. So of course the time continuum hasn't magically been fixed.

I am at peace with my decision, though. Ray and I spent the whole night watching eighties movies from his collection of DVDs. Heathers, The Breakfast Club, The

Outsiders. I think I finally fell asleep during Teen Wolf. He refused to binge on ice cream, which is the quintessential broken heart food, but he did let me make popcorn and poor man's nachos.

Closing my eyes, I take a deep breath and tuck the phone back into its hiding place. Then I venture out to see the family and find out why Ray woke up earlier than me.

Grandpa Joe is wearing khaki cargo shorts and a lime green Hawaiian style shirt with pink flowers all over it while he lays out strips of bacon on a frying pan. Granny wears her pink bathrobe and slippers with her hair tied up in a towel. They're talking about her decision to set up a Pride Month display at the library even though she was warned not to by, and I quote, "that bigoted brat in city services."

"Good morning," Granny says, toasting my arrival by lifting her coffee mug. "Grab some bacon before the guys eat it all. Joe's already eaten most of the first pack."

"I'm making more," Joe says sheepishly. "You know I can't help myself around bacon. It's the crack of breakfast foods."

Granny kisses his shoulder as she walks past him to the coffee maker.

I look around the kitchen, then duck my head into the nearby doorway to find the living room empty. "Where's Ray?"

Granny's brows dip as she pours sugar into the coffee. "He's not with you?"

"No..." In the living room, I look out the front window to find his car gone, which means he wasn't subjected to a random time-traveling event in the middle of the night. Maybe he left me a note. After a quick search around his bedroom, I don't find anything. I even peek into Lindsey's room and check the bathroom mirror—no note. There are no hints that Ray was even here this morning except for the fact that his bed was made.

My grandparents don't seem as concerned about their son being missing as I am.

"Maybe he had to go into work early," Granny says. "Sometimes they'll need him to cover a shift for someone else."

"I don't know why he wouldn't tell me." My uncle's heartbreak is his personal business to tell, so I don't say anything about it, but if they knew he was really hurting when he went to sleep last night maybe they'd be more concerned now.

I grab a piece of bacon from the tray Granny holds out to me. It's maple flavored, but I can't enjoy it because I'm worried about Ray.

"I'll call," she says, crossing the kitchen to where a cordless landline phone is mounted to the wall. A few moments later, her brow furrows as she places the phone back on the receiver. "He's not at work. And he didn't answer his cell."

"He was upset last night." I choose my words carefully, not wanting to reveal too much of his personal life. "I know he's upset about something, and now I'm worried that he'd just leave like this."

"What was he upset about?" Joe asks.

I chew on my lip. "He got in a fight with a friend."

He and Granny exchange concerned glances.

"Why don't you take my car and go look for him?" Granny says.

"Really? That would be great."

"You have your driver's license, right?"

"Yes, ma'am. I'm a great driver."

She smiles and gestures to the key holder on the wall near the garage door. "I'm sure he's fine, honey. Sometimes he likes to go off and be by himself for a while. But you go find him and make sure, okay?"

****

Granny's Jeep Cherokee smells like the synthetic fruity air fresheners she has attached to every air vent. It's not necessarily a bad smell, but it's strong, the full blast of the air conditioning forcing it up my nostrils as I wait for the car to cool down in this summer heat. The car has leather seats, which feel like a lit stovetop griddle on my ass. I pat the pocket on my thigh, an anxious measure to reassure me that my phone is still here. I probably should have left it hidden in Ray's room, but I feel safer with it on me.

Ray's white Mustang is notably missing from the town's one and only shopping center. I know Granny called his work, but I drive around anyway, peeking into the windows at Magic Mark's Pizza to find two employees working there who aren't Ray. Brent's car isn't parked near the music store, either. I consider going inside and asking whoever is there for Brent's number, but it's not like my phone works, and besides, a have a gut feeling that Ray isn't hanging out with Brent right now. My uncle had spent all night hoping for some kind of apology or explanation text from Brent, but it never came.

I only know one other place, and while there's no reason Ray would be at Marci's house, I drive across town to the Castle Estates neighborhood just to make sure. Two decades of expansion in the Greater Houston area have made this luxury home neighborhood just one of many in the acres surrounding it in 2024, but here in the past, Marci's elite subdivision stands alone among fields as far as the eye can see. Ray's car isn't in the driveway, and neither is Marci's Escalade, but I'm guessing she probably parks in the four car garage.

I can't just drive around all day. Granny's car has a full tank of gas but I have no money to refill it. The car idles at the stop sign leading out of Marci's neighborhood. An old Britney Spears song plays softly on the radio, although I guess it's not old right now. I turn it up. Mom would know what to do in this situation. She and Uncle Ray are as close as siblings can get. Nina would know what to do because she's brilliant like that. Even future Uncle Ray would know what to do.

Unfortunately, I'm stuck in this car with only myself, a clueless time traveler.

I drive home.

The old county road shortcut bypasses all of Pine Grove's red lights and stop signs, running parallel to the interstate, miles of maize fields and cow pastures stretching on between the two, equating to sixty miles of nothing. I've driven this stretch of road countless times on the journey from Cypress to Pine Grove to visit Granny. The soft hum of the asphalt comforts me. Before I realize it, an hour has passed, and I'm instinctively tapping the blinker to take exit 35 where the first pit stop before Cypress exists for weary travelers who need a refill at the one tiny gas station, a bite to eat from the Country Corner Diner, or a cheap place to crash at the motel.

My motel is a dirty lump of a building with gray walls, red doors, weeds growing up through the sidewalk, and a broken Cypress Hill Motel sign that serves more as a warning to travelers than a beacon. The letterboard next to the road reads:

VACANCY
$40/NIGHT
CABLE TV!

My mom and uncle bought this facility shortly after I was born using inheritance money they got from their grandparents, ripped it to the studs, and turned it into a tourist attraction that frequently shows up on nerdy websites and Texas magazines. As I stare up at the Cypress Hill Motel, it's hard to see the potential in this gross, worn out place, but somehow they did.

I park by the lamp post, facing room 1. The last time I was in this parking lot was twenty years from now. I only *thought* my life sucked back then. I'd thought losing Jonah was a heartbreak from which I'd never recover. I thought spending my summer working the front counter at the motel would be a tortuous hell compared to spending my nights tucked away in the observatory looking up at the stars like I had planned.

But I actually had it good back then, heartbreak and all. I had an existence that was real, something solid, something rooted in time, space, and the universe. I took it for granted each day. I had Nina. We'd grown up running around this motel like wild, untethered fairy sprites. Letting ourselves into each empty room with my master card key, hiding behind Stormtroopers and crawling over the artificial grass covered hobbit-holes in the Lord of the Rings loft.

We swam in the motel's pool from the moment the mild Houston winter days turned warmer until the heat fell away to cold weather again around Halloween. We talked about crushes and first kisses and weird dreams and what we'd do if someone ever tried to kidnap us.

I feel Nina so strongly in my heart, in my bones. She is a real person, as real as I am. How can I feel this attachment to someone who hasn't even been born yet? Someone who may never be born at all, if I can't find a way to fix everything I've screwed up.

I get out of the car and walk to the back of the parking lot, planting my feet right where they were just a few days ago, facing the highway. Closing my eyes, I look up to the sky, letting the sun pelt me with heat. There's a comfort in feeling the same sun on my skin. Everything is different here on the surface of the planet. But out there, where time is nothing and the fabric of the universe is ever expanding, the stardust is stardust. I am made of stardust, and one day, when my time comes, I'll be stardust once more.

Will any of this even matter?

"Emma?"

When I open my eyes, I see Ray, standing in the gas station parking lot across the road, a small plastic gas jug in his hand.

And he's staring at me like I'm the weird one.

Chapter Twenty

I jog across the rugged two-lane county road, the rumble of the interstate behind me. Ray wears a baggy pair of dark blue Dickie's. There's a dotted bleach stain running down one leg, which he probably got from the dish washing station at work. His old Ataris t-shirt has seen better days. Ray usually looks more put together than this. His hair is even a wavy mess, half pulled back into a tiny ponytail, half slathered on his forehead with sweat.

Ray's car is parked just outside of the gas station, so it's not like he ran out of gas and abandoned his car somewhere along the way.

"What are you doing?" I ask.

"Burning an effigy."

I lift an eyebrow.

"You need gas to get a good fire going," he says, shrugging.

"Why are you way out here?"

"I've always loved this park," he says, nodding toward the rest stop on the other side of the gas station. "Plus, no one knows where to find me here."

I wouldn't really call it a park, although there are half a dozen picnic tables and one covered pavilion that overlooks a man-made lake with a broken water fountain in the middle. In my time, this entire area is one massive Buc-cee's gas station.

"What are you doing?" he asks. "Did you steal Mom's car?"

"Granny loaned me her car, I didn't steal it." I turn back, looking at the motel that's barely recognizable from the place I grew up in. "I'm looking for you," I say. "You left without even telling me. I was worried."

"Sorry." His gaze goes to my leg, where the giant phone-shaped pocket sticks out like a sore thumb. "Are your friends back?"

I shake my head, touching the stretchy fabric on top of my phone. "Not yet."

"Tick tock," he says, handing me the gas jug as he walks by. He pops the trunk of his car open and pulls out a brown paper grocery bag. It looks heavy by the way he carries it with both arms.

It takes me a second to realize he's counting down my deadline to fix everything before my phone dies, not referencing the social media app. He crosses the gas station parking lot, letting himself into the wrought iron gate that surrounds a small rest stop.

This is all concrete in my time. But when a Buc-cee's moves in, it's totally worth paving over the small park that exists now, tucked off the sign of the interstate with only three trees, a few picnic tables, and one sad-looking swing set. Buc-cee's is more than a gas station. It's a gift shop with unique Texan-style gifts, a delicious restaurant with the best BLT you've ever had, and the one place everyone in my school tries to get a job at because they pay well.

I follow him to the closest picnic table. There's a built-in metal barbeque grill next to it, all rusted metal and ashy soot where the charcoals go. Ray drops the bag on top, which lands with a heavy thunk.

"You should just go back to your time tonight," Ray says, reaching over and taking the gas can from me.

"Why would you say that?"

"You'll never be able to change the timeline, and the longer you stay, the more you're messing up the future."

"You don't mean that," I say. "The time continuum is important."

"Nothing is important." He hoists the bag up then dumps it out onto the grill. Ashy soot clouds the air, settling around the odd collection of items. A few CDs, a t-shirt, books. Dozens of pictures and folded letters with Ray's name scrawled on it in a sloppy handwriting.

"Brent," I say softly.

He nods.

"Are you really going to set all this stuff on fire?" I ask, running my hand over the folded up paper notes, an origami swan, a bottle of Coolwater cologne, and Mardi Gras beads that sit on top of a single piece of gum still in the metallic wrapper. I'm sure there's a story that goes with that.

"Yep." To punctuate his point, he pours gasoline on the grill.

I step backward, waving away the pungent fumes. "This is my fault."

"No, it isn't," Ray says so matter-of-factly he sounds like he's totally over the breakup. I don't believe it for one second, but he's doing a good job of faking it. "I was stupid to think we would work. I mean, what was I expecting? We can't even legally get married. Massachusetts just approved gay marriage, but Texas never will."

I bite my tongue. He can get married in the future. And he does. I was the flower girl, so young that I only really remember it by looking at pictures of me toddling down the grassy aisle wearing a silky blue dress. Should I tell him? Should he know that he is married in the future, to a man who is a thousand times better than Brent? I've already screwed up so much of the timeline, I can't risk messing anything else up, even if it might cheer him up in the moment.

I stay quiet.

"I'm glad you're here," he says, setting the gas

jug on a nearby picnic table. With a flick of a match, the effigy goes up in flames.

Ray and I step back to watch from a safer distance. Quiet falls over us as smoke rises in the air and the sentimental items of a fallen relationship warp, blacken, and melt in front of our eyes. My hand presses over the phone in my thigh pocket. All of Jonah's texts are on here, sweet romantic words from a future that will exist if I do nothing to change it. A different future—a past that never happened to me.

My heart squeezes. For so long, the only thing that made me happy was being Jonah's girlfriend. And for days after that soul-crushing moment when he dumped me, I'd wanted him back. I had tied every ounce of my own happiness to Jonah, only to have him cut the tie with a single text.

I'm sorry, but I want to break up.

And now here he is, showering love in my inbox, and all I have to do is set my alarm clock to 2024, go to bed, and wake up to a world where I'm Jonah Pena's girlfriend again.

Quietly, I pull the phone from my pocket and read over his texts again. I touch my phone screen, my fingers sliding over his words. These are the words of a Jonah who shouldn't exist.

I can't take the easy way out. I need Nina back.

And Addy … I guess.

Ray's phone rings from his pocket. He flips it open and puts it to his ear. "Hey, Mom—oh … sorry, I thought you were my mom calling."

When he turns to me, I quickly shove my phone back in my pocket, but he's not looking at that. He holds out his flip phone to me. "Marci wants to talk to you."

Chapter Twenty-One

My eyes widen. He shrugs, his lips flattening in indifference.

I take the phone. "Hello?"

"Hey, girlie. I really need to get your phone number. It took me forever to track down Ray's number."

"I don't have a phone, sorry."

"Damn, you really are living that mysterious girl lifestyle," she snorts, or sniffles. I can't really tell which. Her voice sounds deeper than usual. Is she crying? Or maybe these ancient cell phones just don't have good sound quality.

"What do you need?" I ask as Ray walks up to the effigy, poking things around with a large stick he finds on the ground. He dries the sweat off his face with the inside of his shirt.

"I was hoping you could come over?" Marci says. "Just me and you. Girl time, and all that."

"Sure," I say, eyes wide as I look at Ray who looks just as perplexed as I am, despite not hearing the conversation. "Your house?"

"Yep!" I can hear the smile in her voice. "Hurry up!"

After hanging up the phone, I tell Ray about the mysterious and random invitation.

"The universe just threw you a bone," he says, poking at the fire some more, making sure everything gets gobbled up by the flames. "Hurry over there and get her back with her boyfriend."

"It's weird, though. Why is she calling me instead of one of her real friends? She barely knows me."

"She was the most popular girl when we were in school," Ray says. "I don't think she has any real friends."

****

Marci's house is no less breathtaking the second time I'm here. Ray promised to call his parents and tell them he's okay and that we're going to hang out together for the next few hours, but I don't know why I'm so nervous. I park Granny's car under the covered pavilion at the front of the garage, half-expecting a servant to appear and open my door for me. Marci bounds out a side door instead, all smiles as she rushes out to greet me. I barely have enough time to hide my phone in the glovebox before she's pulling open my car door.

"Hey, girlie!" She bends at the waist, squeezing me into a hug before I've even gotten out of the car. "Thank you so much for coming over. I know we haven't known each other very long, but sometimes you just get a feeling about people, you know?" She smells like cotton candy and sugary vanilla as she steps back, taking my hand and practically pulling me out of the car. "You're cool and sweet and I'm so glad we're friends."

I mentally add *holding hands with my mortal enemy's mother* to the List of Impossible Things that Actually Happened. As if time traveling wasn't insane enough, the universe threw me a massive curveball with Marci. I want so badly to hate this woman who will procreate and ruin my life, but I can't. She's just too damn likable.

But none of that matters. I'm on a mission. I need to convince her to get back with Donovan. I can't lose focus.

While Marci's house isn't exactly a Hollywood movie-star-level of mansion, it's still five times the size of Granny's home, and a million times bigger than my apartment at the Infinity Motel. There's so much open space you can get lost without ever leaving the foyer.

Luckily, she walks me to the curved staircase, past the marble statue of some muscular naked dude, and down the hallway to a bedroom that has the plushest carpet I've ever stepped on. Walking on clouds doesn't even describe it—it's like stepping on memory foam.

"Sorry my room is a little messy," she says, dropping down on a hot pink high heel shoe chair. "I've been stressed lately."

I glance around. Her bed is made, topped with a massive plush Hello Kitty, pink satin pillows with feathery boa trim, and her white padded headboard goes all the way up to the ceiling. I walk over to the French doors that open onto Marci's own personal balcony which overlooks the pool and the horse pasture beyond.

Her furniture is bulky and modern, white wood with little rhinestone lines of trim and a mirror top. Her makeup vanity is incredible. It's probably longer than my entire room is wide, and the mirror has Hollywood style lightbulbs all around it. She has her own bathroom, and I only glance through the open door, but I see a standing shower made of glass walls and a claw-foot bathtub.

I'm not really jealous, just awed. Everyone lives a different life, and this is hers. The life she was born into. The wealth Addy will one day inherit, wealth that comes with a certain expected privilege of getting everything you want. Every*one* you want.

I'm not about to forgive Addy, but maybe I get it, just a little bit.

A rumpled up t-shirt sits on the floor near a door that leads somewhere else with a pair of bunched up socks next to it. That's the only example of messy I can find in Marci's otherwise incredible bedroom, but I smile anyway. "No worries."

"Have a shoe," Marci says, chuckling at her joke as she points to the matching high heel shoe chair next to her. "You want something to drink?"

"I'm fine, thanks."

She leans back in her chair, kicking her feet up onto the ottoman between us. "Would you totally hate me if I immediately start talking about Donovan?"

"Of course not. I kind of thought that's why you wanted some girl time."

Her lips press together, a sad smile that's somehow still glamourous on her. "Yeah, it is." She sighs. "You seemed really invested in getting us back together, and I just really need some perspective. All my friends tell me I'm an idiot for breaking up with him in the first place, but they're biased. They just don't get it."

"Look," I say, leaning forward. These high heel chairs are hideous, but they are comfortable. "I didn't know the whole story when I told you to break up with him ... and I was so not in a place to be giving advice." My chest stretches out into that all too familiar dull ache that comes with thinking of Jonah. "My boyfriend dumped me a couple weeks ago. And I was just angry and hurt and, honestly, I would have told anyone to dump their boyfriend that day."

"Oh, gosh, Emma." Marci reaches out and touches my knee. "I'm so sorry. Whoever your boyfriend was, he's an idiot."

Sure. Jonah is an idiot your future self will follow on Instagram and like everything he posts once he starts dating your daughter.

Knowing the future is an awkward burden to endure. Knowing you shouldn't change any of it is basically torture.

"He left me for another girl." I don't know why I say it, except that the words have been hanging on the edge of my throat, desperate to be vocalized to anyone who will listen. "We were in love and he dumped me for someone else. Someone who used to be my friend. And he told me about it, too! He couldn't just lie like a good person and break up with me—No, he just *had* to tell me he'd fallen in love with A—with her."

I swallow, my heart pounding. Suddenly I want to launch myself out of Marci's balcony window, straight into the pool below.

"What a squid," she says, her lip curling in disgust. "God, I'm so sorry, Emma."

"It's fine." I realize I mean it. It really is fine. "It just wasn't meant to be, I guess … but I don't think that's the case with you and Donovan. I think you two are great together."

Her lips slide to the side of her mouth. "That's what everyone says."

"You should tell him how you feel. I think he'll take you back. He'd be stupid not to."

"He does want me back."

"Really? That's great!" A thousand angels burst out singing in my mind. This is exactly what needs to happen so Nina can come back.

She stands, walking over to her dresser. She takes out a velvet box then hands it to me. "He proposed."

My jaw drops. I lift the box lid and stare at the gorgeous, glittering engagement ring. "When did this happen?"

"Last night."

"This is great news. Why do you look so sad?"

She shrugs. "Donovan wants to be mayor."

"Is that a bad thing?"

"Yes. He wants to be mayor, which means if I marry him, I'll be like my mom, a mayor's wife." She shudders. "I'll be my mother, version two-point-oh."

"And … you don't want that?"

"Hell, no." She groans, turning in a circle in her

room. "I don't want to be the first lady of a small town. I want to be a makeup artist."

"Why can't you do both?"

"Because Donovan wants a trophy wife."

"He can have a trophy wife who is an incredible makeup artist."

"My parents said they won't pay for trade school. They'll pay for a degree I don't want at an expensive college I don't want to attend, but they won't pay for cosmetology."

"So pay for it yourself."

"I don't have any money. I have credit cards that Daddy pays for."

"Take out student loans and pay them off after you graduate," I say. "That's what most people do."

She nods slowly, as if the idea had never occurred to her. "I guess I could..."

"Yes, you can. Do what makes you happy and tell everyone else to piss off."

She laughs, closing the ring box and clasping it to her chest. "Can you imagine me going to cosmetology school? My parents would be so mortified. They'd probably disown me."

"You're twenty-one years old, Marci. You're an adult, so who cares what they think?"

She nods, but her lips press to a thin line, her gaze looking off in the distance. "I don't want to piss off my parents ... but I also want to live my life."

I reach out and squeeze her hand. "Do you love Donovan?"

"Yes." The expression on her face radiates pure love. She opens the ring box again, peering down at it the way most people look at their own children or pets.

I can practically feel Nina and Addy popping back into existence. My entire body prickles with anticipation.

"Good," I say. "Where is Donovan now?"

"He's home. Probably editing the video footage from the pool."

"Go to him. Put that ring on your finger and go to him."

She bites her lip. "It's a perfect ring, don't you think?"

"It's bigger than a jolly rancher. Of course it's a perfect ring."

"It's not *that* big," she says with a playful snort. She puts the ring on her finger, then holds out her hand to admire it. "I'm gonna do it."

"Do it," I say, veiling my own best interests behind the role of encouraging best friend. "Go find him and then marry that boy. And live life on your own terms. Do what makes you happy, Marci."

"I will." Her eyes her a little watery as she admires the ring on her finger. "My parents might go ballistic, but I'll just wait until after the wedding to enroll in school."

"That's a great plan."

"Thanks, Emma." She pulls me into a hug, squeezing tightly. "I knew the universe gave me you for a reason."

"I wouldn't give the universe that much credit," I say. "This is all you. You're choosing to marry the man you love and go after the career you want."

"I'm choosing my fate," she says, lips pressed together. "I like that. I will choose the fate I deserve."

Chills prickle over my skin. I know those words. I've heard them before.

They're the words that caused my world to fall apart.

Chapter Twenty-Two

Addy's Starr Observatory polo shirt still had two creases down the front, like she'd taken it off a shelf five minutes ago and slipped it on, like she was only pretending to work here. Like maybe it was some cruel joke and I actually got the internship of my dreams after all. Her dark hair was pulled into a low messy braid that rested over her shoulder, somehow looking Instagram perfect even in real life where there are no filters and good lighting.

"Thanks for meeting me here," she said.

When I'd gotten the text from Addy to meet her at the observatory, I'd stupidly thought she might have secured me a job, a way to make amends from swooping in and stealing this gig out from underneath me. We hadn't been the closest of friends since high school started, but we had history. All those years of friendship should have counted for something.

As the years went on and we grew from stupid little kids into almost-adults, Addy became increasingly more popular, busy with tennis and student council and organizing fundraisers every other weekend as the socially conscious councilman's daughter. While Addy and I slowly drifted apart, Nina and I had only grown closer, both homebodies who were heavily invested in nerd stuff. Superhero movies, comic conventions … that kind of thing was more attractive than a day of washing cars for some local political fundraiser. But still, Addy was my friend.

And here she was giving me the saddest smile as we sat on the concrete bench just outside of the massive white observatory building, the buzzing of cicadas the only thing breaking the silence between us.

"What's going on?" I asked. The way she was staring at her nails, pushing back her cuticles with a thumbnail made me realize this wasn't a job offer. "Addy?"

"Emma, I'm sorry, but I have something to tell you, and I know you'll be hurt."

"I already know I didn't get the job," I say. This was it—her chance to apologize for taking my job. Maybe even offer to quit so I can step up. After all, what other reason could there be for inviting me to meet her here?

Addy had her mother's sharp jawline, but her father's Italian genes had given her long, chocolatey brown hair. She pushed her ponytail over her shoulder and looked into my eyes.

"Jonah and I are dating."

Even the cicadas seemed to go quiet.

"What?"

She spoke rapidly, the words spilling out almost faster than I could make sense of them. "We didn't start anything while y'all were together, I swear. We wanted to do the right thing, so we waited until he broke it off with you."

"And that's supposed to make me feel better? That my boyfriend didn't cheat, he just rushed to dump me as soon as possible?"

"I'm really sorry it happened like this," she said, her eyes meeting mine. The worst part of all was the real-ass sincerity beneath her gorgeous hazelly-brown eyes. She genuinely felt like shit, and that made me feel two percent better.

But even two percent milk still tastes like crap.

"It didn't have to happen at all," I said, my voice breaking in this pathetically embarrassing way. "You didn't have to steal my boyfriend away from me, Addy!"

She exhaled. "I know it sounds crazy, but Jonah and I—we're soul mates. We just clicked. And I know you don't get it, but you can't just ignore soul mate energy, Emma. We tried to, trust me."

I laughed, a delirious uncanny sound that scared away all wildlife, because suddenly the only sound I could hear was the pounding of my own heart. "That is such a shit excuse, Addy! You stole my boyfriend and you stole my job and now you're here looking all sad as if you can just *apologize* your way to forgiveness?"

"I don't need forgiveness," she said, shoulders stiffening. "I just wanted you to know the truth, and I hope that one day you'll understand when you meet your own soul mate."

I rolled my eyes. "We're seventeen years old. You seriously think Jonah is your soul mate?"

She shrugged. "My parents knew they were soul mates when they were young. Sometimes, it just happens."

"I'm sure stealing my dream job *just happened,* too." I stood up. "Must be so awful for all these amazing things to just fall into your life like this."

"I don't just sit around waiting for things to happen, Emma." She stood, too, her intense gaze somehow making me feel smaller than her when the truth was the opposite. She was short like her mom, and I was tall like mine. "I knew what I wanted, and I went after it. I chose the fate I deserved."

She reached out a hand toward me, but I took a step back. Her head tilted to the side, her smile sad with a hint of condescension that made me want to punch her right in her annoyingly beautiful face.

"If you want happiness, you should do the same thing," she said. "Choose your fate, Emma."

****

What is the point of time travel if instead of preventing my broken heart, I caused it? Either the universe is a cruel, calculating genius, or it's nothing at all. I'm leaning toward the later, but if nothing matters, why does my heart hurt so much? Do the stars hurt when they burn up and collapse into a black hole?

I drive in silence back across town to Granny's house, my mind turning over all the ways my past and my future have collided. In the solitude of the driveway, I check my phone. Ignoring the low battery warning that flashes across my screen, and the blood I taste from biting my lip, I tap on my texts.

I notice the poop emoji before anything else. The air rushes out of my lungs as I tap on Jonah's name, seeing all the original texts back where they belong.

A little sound of relief and pain escapes my lips as I tap back to the messages and scroll down. Addy is also back.

A tear rolls down my cheek. I saved Addy's life—and unlike movie superheroes, I didn't have to destroy the entire city of New York to do it. I just had to destroy my love life and summer internship. Cool. Cool. Cool.

But best of all, Nina's texts are right there where they belong.

Clutching my phone to my chest, I let tears of relief roll down my cheeks. I did it. I fixed the time continuum and brought Addy back. I righted the wrong I caused with a free pizza, brought two lovers back together, unflapped the butterfly's wings and made sure Nina became my best friend. All with eight percent battery life to spare.

As Frodo in The Return of the King says: it's done.

I am going home tonight!

My grandparents are watching the summer

Olympics in the living room, two regular people unaware of the fate-changing adventure I've suffered through over the past week. It's weird to think that when I wake up tomorrow, only one of them will still be alive. I wave as I walk past them.

"Have a good day?" Granny asks.

"Yes, ma'am. Thanks again for letting me use your car."

"I think Ray is in the back yard," Joe says as I walk toward the hall. "Tell him there's some leftover lasagna if he wants it. You, too. It's on the stove."

"Thanks," I say, stopping to watch them for a moment. Granny is curled into Joe's shoulder, his arm around her while they kick back on the couch and enjoy a casual evening together. I envy their love, and regret knowing their future all at the same time. But I got to be here, to witness their love, to be a fly on the wall of a time in the past that no one else ever gets to experience.

Outside, the summer sun is slowly descending into the tree line, but the heat is still ever present, sending an almost instant sprinkling of sweat across my back. The patio table and chairs are empty. I look to the barn, but the door is closed, nothing but darkness escaping through the windows. There's a trampoline out here that I hadn't noticed before, but it's not only empty, it has weeds growing up over the metal poles.

"Over here," Ray calls out. He's lying on a brightly colored quilt spread out over the roof. He waves at me, pushing himself up on his elbows.

"What are you doing up there?"

"Emo shit."

I crawl up the nearby ladder, slowly shifting my body from the metal rails to the roof. It seemed easier from the ground, but now that I've committed, I can't back out now. The roof has a mild slope to it, something that probably wouldn't be scary at all if it weren't several feet off the ground. On all fours, I shuffle over the warm shingles to Ray's blanket. He moves over, making room for me. His eyes seem puffy in the dim lighting. He's still wearing the same ratty clothes from earlier, and the scent of smoke clings to the fabric.

"I hate to ruin your emo shit, but I have amazing news."

"Did you fix the timeline?"

"I did," I say, a goofy-ass grin the size of the Big Dipper on my face. "Addy and Nina are back on my phone, and their texts are the same as from before I came here."

"Nice." He leans back on his elbows, staring up at the deep blue sky. "I knew you'd save the world."

"I wasn't so confident," I say, so overwhelmed with emotions that I might burst out crying again. Too late. I think I am crying. "But not only are Marci and Donovan back together, they're engaged."

"Wow." His teeth drag across his bottom lip, his eyes focused on the sky. "Good job."

I lie back on the quilt, tucking my hands behind my head. The sky is a cloudless deep summer blue. In these long summer days, it won't be dark until just before 9:00. Still, a dozen or more stars are visible in the sky, with the half-moon hanging just over the horizon.

"I get to go home tonight," I murmur. A soft breeze carries my words away, washing them into the vast expanse of the universe.

"I'll miss you, but I won't miss the anxiety I get from having you around."

"The feeling is mutual."

A long moment passes. Ray and I lie here on the roof, eyes on the stars. My mind and body are exhausted. I could probably go down to Lindsey's room and fall asleep right now, so why am I dragging my feet?

"Are you okay?" I ask.

"I'm as okay as I can be for having suffered a heartbreak and the weeklong mindfuck of my yet-to-be-born-niece showing up in my house."

"I think we're going to need some therapy," I say.

He snorts. "I guess the next time I'll see you will be in twenty years."

"You'll actually see me on May 19th, 2007. You and Mom have a pretty funny story about the day of my birth."

"Don't tell me," he says, looking over at me.

"Right. No spoilers."

"How much battery do you have left?"

I take out my phone, the glow lighting up our faces in the ever-darkening sky. "Six percent."

"Shit," he says. "You need to go to sleep, like now."

I scroll through the settings on my phone. "It's estimating eight hours idle time, so as long as I don't use my phone, I'll be okay."

"You still need to go to bed soon," he says, sitting up. "It's a good thing my sister is out of town so you can sneak down to her bed and wake up where you fell asleep."

I reach out and take his hand. "I'm sorry about Brent."

"I'll be okay," he says. It's not exactly a lie, but I can tell he doesn't fully believe it yet.

"Hello," a voice calls out from the darkness below. "There's some dope-ass lasagna down here and you guys are missing out!"

A chill runs down my back. Ray's eyes widen.

Lindsey is home.

Chapter Twenty-Three

This is the absolute worst time for Lindsey to come home from her Zombie Radio tour. My phone is almost dead. I need her bedroom, lest I wake up impaled on Granny's craft supplies in Ray's 2024 bedroom. How exactly do you ask your own mother if you can sleep in her bed when she doesn't even know she's your mother yet?

You don't, that's how.

Lindsey's eye makeup is smudged from a night spent partying with her favorite band and a day spent driving back home. She smells like cigarettes and booze, and her hair is in dire need of washing.

The leftover lasagna smells great, but I have no appetite as I stand in the kitchen with Ray and Lindsey, who is shoveling food in her mouth between telling us about the Zombie Radio tour and how she and her friends ran out of hotel money and had to come back home a few days early.

It's pretty obvious that she's oblivious to the massive awkwardness in the air that's basically suffocating Ray and me. I have to go home tonight or my phone will die. It's hard to pretend to care about her rock band groupie stories when something that heavy is weighing on your shoulders.

Lindsey finishes off her lasagna and tosses the paper plate into the trashcan. "You guys doing anything fun tonight?"

"Just thought I'd time travel into the future," I say.

She snorts. "Sounds fun. I'm gonna go shower the stink off me and then probably pass out. I drove like three hundred miles today. It's been a long day."

When she's gone, I turn to Ray. "What the hell am I supposed to do now?"

"You could sleep on the floor," he whispers as we slip into his bedroom, closing the door behind us. "You'd still wake up in the same room."

Lindsey throws open the door, holding the Cornell pennant that was hanging above Ray's bedroom door the last time I saw it. "Why is this in the trash?"

"Just getting rid of my Cornell stuff," he says, glancing toward the empty space on the wall where it used to be thumbtacked into place. "I'm not going to Cornell anymore."

Lindsey quirks an eyebrow. "Why? Did you get recruited to an even better ivy league school?"

"No."

"You've had this since you were a kid," she says, tossing it at him. "You can't just throw it away. I seriously have to shower now."

With a yawn, she closes the door behind her. Across the hallway, the shower turns on.

Ray tosses the pennant to the floor. The placement of the little Cornell pin-back button pinned to the corner tells me it's the same pennant that's in Ray's apartment in 2024. As a kid, I couldn't wait to grow up and go to college so I could have a cool collegiate pennant, too.

"You're joking, right?" I ask.

"Brent goes to Cornell," he says, his voice resigned. He drops into his desk chair, running his hands through his hair. "I was only going because he goes there."

"No, you were going because it's an incredible architecture school and you've wanted to go there your whole life."

His eyes bunch up on the corners. "How do you

even know that?"

I put a hand on my hip.

"Never mind." He sighs.

I pick up the pennant and lay it flat across his desk. "Raymond Joseph Ross, you are going to Cornell."

His stoic expression is unwavering. "I'm not going to Cornell."

"Yes, you are. You can't give up your future because of some guy."

"It's just a stupid tchotchke I got when I was in fifth grade," he says, shoving the pennant into the metal trash bin under his desk. "It's not important."

I kneel down and take it out of the trash. "It's important to me."

"The important thing is that you should be going to sleep. Like, now."

I start to object, but he stops me. "I don't want to hear about the future, Emma."

If my uncle were to drop out of Cornell before school starts in the fall, my life as I know it won't exist anymore. It would mean he never meets Charlie, never gets the architecture degree that inspires him to build the Infinity Motel into a nerd paradise, and I never get to grow up in it. Only the universe knows what our lives would be like if he doesn't go to Cornell. I refuse to let the universe reveal that future to me.

"You can't give up your dream school because of a broken heart."

"Emma, listen. This isn't something you can fix. I've felt this way for a while. I think I've known I wasn't going to Cornell for a long time now, and this Brent thing just helped me make the choice." He puts his hands on my shoulders. "I would have made this choice with or without you."

Chapter Twenty-Four

I wonder if the universe keeps tabs on how many times Star Wars has saved someone's life. When Lindsey got out of the shower, Ray somehow managed to convince her that having an impromptu Star Wars movie marathon in his bedroom was a great idea. Only six movies exist in 2004, and they decide to watch them in chronological order instead of movie release date order. Six movies will be plenty of time for Lindsey to fall asleep on the piles of pillows and blankets we spread out on the floor in Ray's bedroom.

When that happens, I'll slip into her room and go to sleep. I'm too amped up to focus and before I know it, Attack of the Clones is over, and Ray is popping in the DVD for Episode IV: A New Hope.

I glance over at my future mom. She's curled up on a bean bag, a half-eaten bag of popcorn resting in her lap. I sit up, quietly pushing the blanket off my lap. She stirs, blinking a few times. Dammit.

"I gotta pee," I whisper. It's half an hour until midnight, and while I have no proof that midnight triggers the time travel thingy on my phone, I really wanted to be asleep before now. Will I time travel instantly? Or not until the alarm clock goes off at 6:00 in the morning?

In the bathroom, I take the world's most anxious pee. My whole body is vibrating. From lack of sleep, fear, or guilt, I don't know. Ray told me not to tell him anything about the future, but Cornell is his future.

I wander through the darkened house, stopping when I notice movement from outside, just beyond the glass patio doors. A soft glowing orange dot hovers in the air. It's Joe, smoking a cigar. He nods at me.

I slide open the door and step out into the crisp night air, the sweet smoky smell of the cigar wrapping itself around me like a warm blanket.

"Dot hates these things," he says, flashing me a grin. "She says they make me smell like an old carpet store, whatever that means, so I only smoke them when she's not around."

"It's kind of a cool smell," I say, inhaling the rich musk. No one smokes cigars in my time. Not my family, and not my friends. Some of them vape, but it's not even close to being the same thing.

"Something on your mind?" he says, leaning over the wooden porch railing. He waves the smoke away from me.

"I'm stuck in a conundrum," I say. "I want to do something for my friend, but they don't want me to help them because they think they should figure out their own problems. But I know that it's the right thing."

"So do it," he says.

I sigh, leaning on my elbows. "If I do the thing, it'll be going against what they want."

"The person you're talking about," he says, taking a long puff from the cigar. "Are they in your bubble?"

"What bubble?"

With the cigar in his fingers, he holds out his hands, palms facing inward. "Your personal bubble. Family, close friends. The people who *really* matter to you."

"Yes," I say. "He matters a lot."

"Then you gotta do what's best for him."

"How do I know it's the right thing to do?"

"Life is too short," he says softly. "And the world is too big. You can't single-handedly feed every hungry person. But you can make sure those closest to you eat. You can't heal everyone, but you can help those you love. All we have is our bubble." He makes that hand motion again, the cigar hanging from his lips. "You gotta protect that bubble."

"Thanks," I say. "For everything. I really appreciate you letting me stay here this week."

"It's no problem, Emma. You're in my son's bubble, which means you're also in mine."

All my anxiety drifts away like the cigar smoke fading into the night sky. I look up at him, this tall, punk rock guy who would have been the best grandfather. I know why Granny's voice gets that soft lilt to it every time she talks about him. I know why she's never even thought about dating anyone else. He's her soul mate.

I throw my arms around him, squeezing tightly for a second before pulling away. "I'm really glad I got to meet you."

I tip toe back into Ray's bedroom. His beaming smile glows red and blue from the lightsaber battle on the TV screen. He holds up both hands, thumbs out and mouths "she's asleep" while nodding toward his sister. Lindsey's mouth is slightly open, her chest rising and falling in a deep slumber.

I pull my phone from my pocket. Five percent battery left. Ray hovers over my shoulder while I open the clock app and click on the alarm. I set the time for 6:00 in the morning, then scroll the date all the way up to 2024. Surprisingly, the date doesn't go any higher than that, and it doesn't go any lower than 2004. It doesn't matter, though. I have no desire to travel anywhere else outside of the time continuum.

"I guess this is goodbye," Ray whispers.

I peer up at him as shadows light and darken his features. His hair is all messy, his eyes ringed with dark circles. "You once asked me if you're happy in the future," I whisper. "I need you to know that you are happy."

His lips part, but he stands here frozen in front of me, a million unasked questions hiding just behind his eyes. I press my hand to his chest, lean in, and talk quickly so I won't lose my nerve. "You are happy in the future. You're a Cornell graduate, and you're my openly gay Uncle Ray, and you're happy."

A tear rolls down his cheek, his lips quivering.

A tear rolls down my cheek, too. "It's the only way I've ever known you."

With that, I slip into Lindsey's room, close the door, and fall on top of her bed, my phone clutched tightly in my hand. For one brief moment, I worry I won't be able to fall asleep.

But then exhaustion takes over and I close my eyes, surrendering my fate to whatever the universe has planned next.

Chapter Twenty-Five

A soft vibration pulls me from a deep sleep, the buzzing growing louder with each passing second. I blink awake, arm flying out to silence my phone from the nightstand. It's early. So impossibly early in the morning. Even the sun is barely up. I close my eyes as the soft, wonderful feeling of sleep washes over me again.

My body feels heavy, like my bones have been replaced with concrete. I roll over in bed, yawning so hard it makes my jaw ache. That's when I hear it.

Breathing.

My eyes fling open. It's Nina, passed out beside me, curled up in floral sheets, her dark hair a mess all over the floral print pillowcase.

Nina!

I roll over, smashing my face to hers, wrapping my arms tightly around her so she doesn't disappear. "I'm so glad you're here."

"Ugh," Nina groans, eyes squeezing shut as she tries to shrug off my hug. "It's too early."

"No, it's the perfect time," I say, resting my head on her shoulder. "It's 6:00 in the morning on the perfect day, in the perfect year."

"Are you high?" she mutters, her voice groggy from sleep as she stirs awake. She sits up, rubbing her eyes. "I was having a perfectly good dream until you assaulted me awake."

"It's time for donuts, remember?"

"Oh, yeah." She nods, then pulls a hair tie off her wrist and wrangles her hair into a low ponytail. "That seemed like such a great idea last night, but now I just want to sleep for infinity more hours."

"I'm so glad you're my best friend."

Nina smiles, tilting her head to the side. "What happened to you?"

"I time traveled to the year 2004 and almost ruined everything, but then I had to make sure Addy was born so you'd still be my best friend."

"Right," she says, nodding as she stands up and slides her feet into her sandals. "My dream wasn't that cool. I dreamed we were in Austin eating limitless tacos and for some reason they were using an avocado skin as the taco shell, but it didn't taste bad." She curls her lip. "Weird."

I laugh. "I love you, best friend."

"I love you, too," she says, stretching her arms over her head. "Let's sneak out of here and get donuts."

While my phone charges in the car, I can't help but feel wary of it. It gets signal now, and I even got two new junk emails overnight, but it's still a time machine, unless of course, everything that just happened was some kind of dream. I sneak glances at it while we drive to the square donut place that's just down the road, located in a shopping center that used to be an empty field. We order a dozen assorted donuts, and Nina connects her phone to my car and plays songs from our shared BFFs playlist.

Back at Granny's, we sneak inside, start a pot of coffee, and set up the table for an elaborate breakfast. I keep looking around, wishing for some kind of hint that everything I'd just experienced wasn't some fantastical lucid dream.

Granny is thrilled with our donut surprise, but seems even more impressed that we were able to wake up before noon. I can't stop staring at her while we sit around the kitchen table, eating and singing along to showtunes. Her white-blonde hair is frizzier and a little shorter. She still wears her signature red lipstick every day, but now that she's retired she's more of a leggings and t-shirt kind of woman.

The doorbell rings.

"Good morning," Uncle Ray calls out as he lets himself inside the front door. "Surprise visit from your favorite son."

Uncle Ray's dark hair is cut short, parted on the left, and neatly trimmed along the edges. He's leaner, taller, and walks with a confident swagger that, until now, I assumed he was born with. There are slight wrinkles in the corners of his eyes, and two creases running horizontally across his forehead. But his eyes, those dark pools of emo punk rock and nerd core are the same. Exactly the same as always.

"You are my only son," Granny says, giving him a dismissive wave. "That means you're also my least favorite."

"Ouch." He puts a hand to his chest, wincing.

"The girls got me donuts this morning," she says, holding up her apple-filled pastry. "Come get one."

"Not this one," Nina says, cupping her hands in the air over the maple bacon donut. "I will have to fight you if you try eating this one."

"I'll take a donut, but I can't stay long," he says. His eyes find mine from across the room. "We have a little emergency at the motel and I need to grab Emma for a few hours."

"She's on vacation," Granny says, frowning.

"It won't take long." He reaches across the table and grabs a chocolate iced donut. "I'll have her back by lunch. Emma, I know you've only been away from the motel for one night, but it feels like, oh, I don't know … twenty years."

My eyes widen.

He smirks.

My chair screeches across the tile as I stand up.

"I'll get my shoes on."

Chapter Twenty-Six

Ray's sports car rumbles as he backs out of the driveway. It's an Audi, white with black leather seats, the dream car he'd waited years to own. I sit here riding shotgun next to him like I've done so many times in my life, but it feels surreal now. We're at the end of the neighborhood before I find my voice.

"So it was real?"

Eyes on the road, he says, "It was real."

We pull up to a red light that was a stop sign twenty years ago. Uncle Ray looks over at me, wearing an expression I can't decipher.

"It was real," I say again.

"You think *your* mind is blown? I had to wait twenty years for this moment."

I stare at him until the light turns green. I can see the remnants of the boy he used to be, all grown up and matured. A shiver runs through me. "Tell me everything."

"Well…" He draws in a deep breath and hits the gas, shifting swiftly through the gears. "When I woke up the next morning, you were gone. I told the family you had gone back to live with your family who had just come back to town. And then I spent a couple years wondering if I had just hallucinated the whole thing, which could have been possible because I was going through a rough time, mentally. But a few years later, Lindsey had a baby and named her Emma. I was so excited to meet you, but I was up at Cornell and couldn't afford a plane ticket. In my hurry to get to the hospital, I accidentally got on the wrong Greyhound bus and ended up in California."

I grin. "That's it. That's the funny story I told you

about."

"Really?" He shakes his head, eyes on the road. "Time travel is *wild*. So anyway, later on, Marci and Donovan's family put out this huge ad in the paper congratulating them on their newborn baby. When I saw they had named their spawn Addyson, I knew it had to be real."

I can't stop staring at him. In the past twenty-four hours, I've spent time with teenage Uncle Ray and adult Uncle Ray. I've been right here, within touching distance of two versions of the same person. It's trippy. It's weird. It's … real.

"Here's a question," Ray says, flashing me a cheeky grin while he drives. "Who is my husband, in your timeline version of events?"

"Charlie. His name was Charlie Rosemary, but he hated his last name so much he demanded to take yours when y'all got married."

"Huh," he laughs. "So my theory is correct."

"What's your theory?"

"The time continuum wasn't split off—it was just … looped. So long as you went back to the exact time you left, the experience you had just looped back on itself. My timeline was forever altered because I met you, but yours just picked up where it left off. We avoided the 'meeting yourself in the future' paradox because there is no alternate version of you. You left your timeline, but then you came right back and no time had passed here in 2024."

"What nerdy ass sci-fi book gave you that theory?"

He laughs. "It's my own theory."

"Maybe you should write a sci-fi novel about a girl who goes back in time and prevents her mortal enemy from being born. You know, someone slightly less ethical than me."

"I'll title it: *The Time Traveling Teenager,* subtitle*: The Ex-girlfriend's Revenge.*"

I relax back into my seat, letting the relief of being back in my own time seep into my pores. I hadn't realized until just this moment that the last week had me so anxious my body had basically calcified into a ball of anxiety. Now, things are back in place. The world outside these car windows looks just like I remember it.

"So what was it like? What was *I* like all these years?"

He shrugs, tapping the blinker and changing lanes. "You're Emma. You're my niece. We have a great relationship. Sometimes when we worked the graveyard shift at the motel together, I'd want to ask you if you knew anything about time travel, but I didn't because of course you wouldn't. If the timeline worked the way I suspected, you wouldn't know anything about what happened until today, the day you return to your own time."

"So you just ... waited? For twenty years?"

"Yep."

"Oh, gosh. I'm sorry." Outside, my little part of the world feels a whole lot bigger. We have fast food chains and new subdivisions and roads that are four lanes instead of two. So much has changed in the last twenty years. The implications of what has happened drops on my soul like a lead weight. "Ray, I'm so sorry."

"For what?"

"I had to suffer through a week of time travel, but you've lived with this for twenty years."

"It was worth it. Because if you hadn't showed up when you did, I wouldn't have made the choices I made. I wouldn't have gone to Cornell. I definitely wouldn't have the motel. Everything that happened in my life, everything good in my life, is because you time traveled."

"But that means I did change the time continuum. Isn't that the opposite of what I was supposed to do?"

He shrugs. "Hell if I know, kid."

I didn't notice when he took an exit, but we're no longer on the interstate that leads to the motel. We're on a county road now, the one that leads way out to the middle of nowhere, where the city lights don't reach.

"This isn't the way to the motel."

My uncle's lips press together in an awful attempt to suppress his shit-eating grin. "What? Are you sure?" he says, faking innocence. "Hmm, wonder where we're going…"

"The only thing out here is endless woods, wildlife, and the one place that doesn't want me working for them."

The observatory.

"You sure about that?"

"Addyson got the internship, not me… Unless?"

"No, she did," he concedes. "And you'll still have to work with her, because although I'm amazing, I'm not a miracle worker."

"I don't understand."

"In college when Lindsey and I inherited that money we spent on the hotel … I decided to invest a little bit of it."

I quirk an eyebrow.

"You were pretty obsessed with that phone you had in 2004, and it had the little apple logo on the back and well…" He points a finger in the air. "Apple stock has gone up *a lot* in twenty years."

"You didn't!"

He nods, a wicked smile dancing across his face. "Oh, I did. And I didn't touch the money at all until this week because I wanted to make sure you came back and everything was fine. So anyway, I'm kind of rich now." He shrugs. "Not politician rich or anything, but enough to make a large donation to the observatory."

We turn off the winding gravel road and park next to the only other car in the small lot. The air smells sweeter in the woods than in town. Like pine trees and summer mixed together. Uncle Ray and I walk the trail that leads from the small parking lot into the woods, winding its way to the tall man-made grassy hill where the observatory sits surrounded by woods that are hundreds of years old. The white domed building looms in the distance, a mechanical beacon of humanity's hope and curiosity.

"So what does your donation mean?" I ask. The observatory is notoriously underfunded, which is why their internships are unpaid.

He wiggles his eyebrows. "Now they have more money for more programs, and Julie—that's the director of operations—we're on a first name basis," he says, winking at me, "was thrilled to hear that I have a niece who would be the perfect intern to head up all of these exciting new things. She wants to meet you today."

"You *bribed* my way into an internship? What if you piss off the universe?"

"First of all, I like to think of it as a nice philanthropic donation and a happy coincidence, not a bribe."

He looks up to the sky, looping his fingers together behind his head. "Secondly, the universe didn't give us a time travel handbook. You saved me when you went back in time, and I decided to save you in return."

He's quiet for a minute, eyes up at the stars which are hidden from the glow of the morning sun. I look up, too, wondering what he's waiting for. Nothing happens.

"See? The universe seems cool with it."

We climb the steep sidewalk to the observatory, the sweet scent of wild honeysuckle filling my lungs. I stop at the top of the hill and look out at the forest beyond the clearing. "Uncle Ray?"

"Hm?" he says, standing next to me.

"Since you're rich now, can I have some money?"

"What for?"

"I want to buy a new phone and destroy this one."

"You're not tempted to charge the battery, go back in time, and alter history to become a billionaire and get Jonah back?"

I shake my head. "I have the things I want. Maybe not everything, but I have my bubble. I have the things that matter."

He grins. "I think the universe would appreciate that."

"Me, too."

The observatory door is a massive, heavy thing that groans as Ray pulls it open. Darkness and cold air rush out to greet us. I used to sit on the motel roof at night, gazing up at the stars, wondering if my future was written on them. Visits to this very observatory made me feel closer than ever to the vast, ever-expanding galaxy that I call home. Maybe that's why I love it so much. We are tiny, the universe is huge. And yet, we belong here. We are a part of this.

But it never fails that once I step back from the viewfinder and the black domed walls of the observatory come back into focus, I realize I am made not only of stardust, but of the memories of every moment that's made up my life so far. Maybe my future has been decided. Maybe it's all up in the air. I don't know what the future holds.

But I do know one thing. Addy can have Jonah.

I'll take the stars.

CHEYANNE YOUNG

Evernight Teen ®

www.evernightteen.com